HER TIGER TO TAKE

TIGER SHIFTERS 4

KAT SIMONS

T&D PUBLISHING

HER TIGER TO TAKE

Published 2015 by T&D Publishing
Cover art design © 2014 and 2019 The Killion Group
Interior book design © 2019 T&D Publishing
ISBN-13: 978-1-944600-15-0 (Trade Paperback Edition)

This is a work of fiction. All of the characters, places, organizations, and
events portrayed are either products of the author's imagination or are used
fictitiously. Any resemblance to actual persons, living or dead, business
establishments, events, or locales is entirely coincidental.

First printing: April 2019
For information, contact T&D Publishing www.TandDPublishing.com

For my boys

Nikolai Chernikov knew the woman was a tiger shifter the instant she stepped into his diner. He'd felt her the moment she came into town. No tigers lived anywhere near Eirene, which was why he'd settled here five years ago.

Worse still, the tiger invading his territory was *her*. Tatiana Loban-Gupta. She was more dangerous to him than all the rest of his people combined.

She sat at the counter and glanced around the cozy space, taking in the bustling breakfast crowd. For several moments, Nick couldn't think past his raging heartbeat. She was stunning. Golden blonde hair, dark brown eyes, perfect heart-shaped lips, and a figure so lush it made his mouth water.

She was even more beautiful than she'd been six years ago, the first time he'd seen her. They hadn't met then. She hadn't even noticed him, much to his relief. But that moment was fixed in his memory.

He'd been at the elders' compound in West Virginia, stalking through the corridors deep in thought after a meeting with his grandmother, where she'd once again tried to talk him into returning to the Mate Run. He'd walked into a large, open atrium and looked up.

There Tatiana stood with two males and a female, smiling, laughing, and talking as if the world hadn't just turned upside down. Her scent washed over him, a mix of honeysuckle, female, and her basic essence, robbing him of breath. His pulse hammered hard. Something about her scent called to him on a basic level, beyond anything he'd experienced before; primal and insistent. His tiger lifted its head and growled.

She wasn't just beautiful and sexy. She wasn't just a rare and delectable female tiger shifter. His tiger insisted she was *his*.

Only a moment passed, a few heartbeats, then he'd turned and escaped to his room at the complex, running from the spark of electricity he'd felt for her. He'd tried to tell himself it was for her own good. He was one of the infamous Chernikov brothers. No tigress in her right mind wanted to be saddled with him. No tigress gave the Chernikov boys a second glance.

She'd grown even curvier over the years, curves that had nearly brought him to his knees four months ago when she'd come out of nowhere and introduced herself. His damned bad luck to have been at the elders' compound again at the exact same time she'd been there. He'd managed to avoid her for six years. And all that careful avoidance had gone to hell.

Damn her, what was she doing here? Didn't she know better?

His tiger raised its head, scenting the air and absorbing her deliciously unique fragrance. That scent had haunted him since he'd first picked it up. The tiger in him saw a mate.

The man in him saw trouble.

He waited for her to order coffee from Jane before he came out of the kitchen to greet her. He had to settle himself, control his reaction, or he was likely to scare off all his customers and ruin the comfortable life he'd built for himself here.

As soon as he stepped into the main room, her gaze locked on to his. She smiled, just a little, and raised her coffee mug to her lips as she watched him approach.

Fuck. He was in serious trouble.

"Tatiana," he greeted her from the opposite side of the counter. Safer to have at least some obstacle between them, even if it was only the flimsy barrier of wood and Formica. "What brings you here?"

"You."

Well, she didn't mince words. He liked that about her. "You shouldn't have come."

"What else could I do? You've been avoiding me for months now. You ignore my letters and emails. You didn't leave me much choice."

"You could have stayed away."

"You know better than that."

No, he didn't. But that wasn't a conversation they could have in public. "You want something to eat?"

"What's good?"

"Everything. My omelets are really popular."

She wrinkled her nose and shivered. "No, thanks. Maybe just a side of bacon?"

He hid a smile and nodded. For some reason, most tigers hated eggs. He wasn't one of them, but obviously, Tatiana didn't share his taste.

"Be right back." He felt her gaze along his spine all the way back to the kitchen.

Every muscle was stiff and tight as he worked to contain instincts better kept in check. His tiger didn't want to listen to civilized logic, but giving in to those thoughts would be disastrous.

He'd moved to this isolated little town in Colorado and stayed as far away from his own people as was possible for five years. Occasionally, he saw his brothers when they stopped in to visit. But they had their own lives, so emails and phone calls had become the default. Outside of that situation four months back with Mitch and his new fiancée and the subsequent trip Nick had had to take to the elders' compound, he hadn't been around his own kind in a long time.

Which suited him and the other tigers.

Tatiana being here was going to bring down a world of trouble onto his head. The kind of trouble he'd gone out of his way to avoid. The older he got, the more he just wanted peace. Tatiana was the exact opposite of peace. She was excitement, chaos, passion, reckless abandon. And despite what his tiger kept telling him about her, he did not want to go back to fighting every single day of his damned life.

He finished the bacon but sent the plate out to her via his waitress Jane.

He was a coward.

Scrubbing his hands over his face, he let out a quiet groan. "Fuck."

He stared at the wall for a long moment, and then gave in to necessity. He couldn't ignore her anymore. He couldn't pretend she meant nothing to him. But he couldn't have her either, and she needed to get that through her thick skull.

Which meant they had to talk.

But damn, if that wasn't going to be the hardest conversation of his life.

Tatiana worked hard to keep her knee from bouncing as she ate her way through the plate of bacon. She was putting everything on the line being here, but she didn't have a choice. She couldn't continue on as she'd been indefinitely. She had to talk Nick into returning to the Mate Run, *her* Run.

She assumed a relaxed pose and tried not to let her nerves show, but her stomach danced with both giddy excitement and dread. In an attempt to distract herself, she studied the little diner Nick owned. It was a charming place with bright walls, polished wooden floors, and tables decked out with the kind of paper coverings kids could draw on. She smiled as one little boy, probably no older than two, scribbled furiously on the paper with two different colored crayons, then raised his hands in triumph to present his masterpiece.

The sight tightened a band around her chest and she had to look away.

Despite what the others said, she *did* want children. She'd always wanted them. Lots of them.

But she refused to mate with just any tiger, and until she'd caught Nick's scent four months ago, she'd despaired of ever finding a suitable mate. Every male who'd come forward to participate in her Mate Run fell short. She tried to keep an open mind, but when the time came to choose, she just…kept running. The idea of any of them catching her filled her with dread.

You weren't supposed to dread being with the man who might possibly be the father of your children.

The elders had tried to help, and Tiana had honestly tried to select a potential mate. Her Run had been opened to males from around the US, a much larger pool than normally participated. Usually only the males located near a female's territory took part in her Run. But then, usually the females knew who they wanted before they even started to run.

For reasons she'd never been able to understand, *none* of the tigers she'd met did anything for her. She wasn't trying to be obstinate or difficult. She just wanted to *want* the man she'd spend three days having sex with, and so far, not one of them had sparked that chemical, basic lust in her.

She'd started to worry about herself. Maybe something was wrong with her. Maybe she was broken.

Then she'd caught Nick's scent and every nerve in her body came to life. Her heart raced, her stomach tightened, her lips tingled. She drank in that delicious smell and all the wonderful sensations swamping her body like a woman deprived of water for years. She'd thought the scent seemed vaguely familiar, but she knew she'd never had this reaction to another tiger before, so it had to be someone new to her.

She was so excited to actually feel lust for a tiger it wouldn't even have mattered what he looked like. The fact that he turned out to be gorgeous was a bonus—tall, well-muscled, light brown hair, green eyes, strong features. She'd very nearly jumped into his arms the minute she'd seen him. A combination of relief and lust had rolled through her in delightful waves.

Until she'd discovered he was one of the Chernikov brothers.

Worse, he was the oldest Chernikov. Nikolai—or Nick, as he preferred—hadn't taken part in a Mate Run for more than ten years. And no one wanted him to return to it.

Except her.

As far as Tiana was concerned, the others could just get over it. Tiger shifters were on the brink of extinction. Too many males, not nearly enough females, and the numbers dropping no matter what they did. The institution of the Mate Run had staved off societal chaos. It was the only way a male could earn a rare female. During a females estrous, several males gathered to chase and compete for her. They ran until one of the males "caught" the female—the male she allowed to catch her. Once a male got a female pregnant during the Run, the couple was allowed to stay together permanently if they wanted. But the Run hadn't done anything to increase the number of female births.

It was better for their people if she mated and had children. If the mate she wanted was considered the dregs of the tiger world, well, so be it. He was her choice.

The problem was convincing him of that.

When he finally came back out of the kitchen, her heart jumped and her pulse sped. His scent wrapped around her like a delicious aphrodisiac, and she actually had to work to keep from crawling over the counter to get to him. She was two weeks away from her next reproductive cycle. She had two weeks to convince him to join her in that Run.

Failure was not an option.

"Where are you staying?" he asked without preamble.

"I've got a room in the motel near the highway." She couldn't help herself when she said, "Why? Are you offering me a better option?"

His mouth turned down and she heard his faint growl. "That's not gonna happen, and you know it."

"I know no such thing."

"Tatiana…"

His warning tone only stoked the flames dancing along her nerves. She'd never wanted a man so much in her life. Nick might try, but he was not getting away from her.

She nodded to the kitchen. "When will you be finished?" She cut her gaze to the not-so-subtle stares of the diner's clientele. "It's probably better if we talk in private."

She actually saw his throat work as he swallowed, and she had to suppress a satisfied smile. His desire flavored his scent, adding a musky punch that only excited her more. But Nick was no desperate cub she could command with the flick of her hand. If she rushed things, he'd shut her out completely, and she'd lose her only chance at ever having a mate.

His gaze wandered over the dining room as he considered his options. Finally, he said, "The breakfast rush ends in another hour. We'll talk then."

He turned his back to her and returned to the kitchen, leaving her as nervous as a teenager waiting on her first date.

One hour. She had one hour to rally all her arguments and logical points to convince him to chase her.

But as she watched him walk away, her brain simply refused to work. All she could think about was dragging him back to her motel room and fucking him until the world ended. That wasn't an option, not if she wanted any hope of a family with him. She was playing a dangerous game even being here. If any of the others found out…

No, she wouldn't consider that now. She had to focus on convincing him to come back to the Run. Every other problem could wait.

CHAPTER TWO

When the hour was up and Nick knew he couldn't stall anymore, he threw on his coat, stalked out to the dining room, and motioned her to follow with a sharp hand gesture. He knew it was rude but didn't really care. She'd invaded his space, endangered his peace, and worse, she made him long for something he couldn't have. A part of him wanted to hate her for that.

She didn't argue or glare at his behavior. She simply sauntered after him, confident and relaxed.

He could feel the stares of the remaining customers. In fact, the diner was still full, despite the fact that it was past the breakfast hour and most of those people had places to be. The reason he loved Eirene was because the towns-people believed in letting others have their privacy. That didn't stop them from being curious.

Once outside, Nick realized he had a problem. There wasn't anywhere in town he and Tatiana could go to have the kind of privacy they needed. Any of the public spaces would be like his diner—the entire town would watch and listen in. Anywhere private was entirely too dangerous. Being alone with Tatiana was a temptation he didn't want to risk.

Unfortunately, he didn't have an option.

With an irritated grunt, he said, "This way," and led her to his small house, only a short walk from the diner.

The surrounding mountains were beautifully coated with fresh snow, the pine trees a dark break in the swaths of white. The rocky path behind his diner wound through a small copse of trees and gave the feeling of moving deeper into the woods, even though his house was only a few hundred yards off Main Street. He loved that sense of peace and isolation while still being close to the bustle of his little town. His town. This place was more home to him than anywhere else he'd ever lived. He felt...*right* here, like he belonged.

He breathed in the pine and snow scents and caught Tatiana's honeysuckle deliciousness mixing with it all.

Damn it all to hell.

He stalked onto his front porch, stomped the snow off his boots, and went inside—all without talking to her. He tossed his coat onto the hook by the door and motioned her to his little living room to the right. "Sit. You want some-thing to drink?"

"No, thank you." She ambled into his home, making a circuit of the living room as she stripped out of her coat.

Watching her remove any clothing at all made his pulse pound. She was still fully dressed in a tight turtleneck and jeans. But she might as well have been naked for all the barrier those clothes were to his imagination. Her scent filled his head, overriding all his common sense. Having her here was stupid. Why the hell hadn't she stayed away?

"Why the hell did you come?" he asked aloud.

"You know why. I want you to run."

"I don't run anymore."

She faced him. "Start again."

"Why?"

"Because I want you."

Damn her and her honesty. How was a man supposed to resist that statement from a beautiful woman? "Choose someone else."

"I've been running for three years. Don't you think I would have chosen someone else if there was anyone else? You're it, Nick. Get used to it."

God, how he wanted to believe that. He wanted to just give in and take what she was offering. But for him, it wasn't that simple. "Do you have any idea what you're getting into with me? How you'll be treated? The affect this could have on your children?"

She eased down onto his couch and stared up at him with those fantastic brown eyes, and it was all he could do to stay in the living room doorway.

"You're not broken. You're not a genetic disaster. There's nothing wrong with you, and there's no reason we shouldn't be together."

"Tell that to the others. You don't want me, Tatiana," he said, quietly. "You don't want the trouble you'll get."

"Stop trying to tell me what I do and don't want, you ass," she snapped.

He raised his brows.

She looked away, her cheeks pink. "There's nothing wrong with you," she insisted.

"My mother killed herself and my father was confined for killing a human. There's plenty wrong with me." In fact, the only reason he and his brothers were even allowed to run was because his grandmother was a powerful elder, and she'd negotiated that concession for her grandsons when her son went into confinement.

Tatiana scowled. "You were what, nine years old when that happened?"

"Doesn't matter. Most of the tigers see my mother's suicide as a sign of mental weakness. Then my father, in his grief, kills a human man because the woman he was beating bore a vague resemblance to my mother. More proof of mental weakness. And years later, he has to be confined again for stalking a human woman who might have looked something like my mother. Mental weakness. On both sides of my family. There's a reason no other tigress ever let me catch her during the years I took part in the Run."

"A lot of males who don't have your history never manage to get a mate. It's a matter of numbers, not biology."

"Not in my case. I was actively snubbed. And there's only so long a man can tolerate that before he walks away."

His last Run had been the final insult in a long line of humiliations. The tigress came right out and told him she didn't want to "endanger" her future children's mental health by mating with someone like him. That incident had been enough for Nick. He'd refused to run again—despite pressure from his grandmother.

Tatiana launched up off the couch and approached him. "I *won't* snub you, damn it. I wouldn't be here if I didn't intend to let you catch me."

She stopped so close he could feel the heat of her skin along his and his stomach muscles tightened. Too close. She was too close.

"If anyone finds out you're here," he said, "it won't matter what you want. I'll be banned from running."

"You left me no choice."

"There's always a choice."

"That's my point."

Fuck. She had him so wound up, the very argument he was trying to use against her worked against him, as well.

"I've made my choice," he said, his voice gravel rough and almost an octave deeper.

"It's the wrong one," she said, edging closer.

"Tatiana…" But even he didn't believe the low growl was the warning he'd meant it to be.

She touched his cheek with gentle fingertips. "Nick. Please."

He closed his eyes. How could he resist her soft plea? How could he turn away from something he wanted so damned much when it was being offered freely?

His eyes were still closed when he felt the warmth of her breath against his lips. He kept his eyes closed, his body motionless as she pressed her mouth to his in a tentative, searching kiss. Every muscle in his body tightened as need roared through him, a need he'd been suppressing for six long years.

Fuck it.

He wrapped his arms around her waist and deepened the kiss, taking what he'd wanted since the first moment he'd seen her. She melted against him, her full breasts a delicious pressure against his chest. Her scent enveloped him, mixing with his own until a new, unique combination swirled in eddies around them. So perfect a flavor he was surprised it hadn't always been a part of his life.

She tunneled her fingers through his hair, keeping him close. Though at this stage, he wasn't going anywhere. She tasted salty, sweet and tangy all at once and he couldn't get enough. He dropped his hands to the swell of her beautiful ass and pulled her tighter against his erection. Her softness was irresistible. He squeezed and caressed until he was panting with a desperation that surprised him.

He broke from the kiss to taste more of her, nuzzling her soft hair aside and pushing at her shirt to get at the delicate skin along her throat. Her pulse pounded beneath his lips, further firing his need. When he licked her skin, she moaned, and his entire body reacted.

"God, Tatiana…" He barely recognized his own voice. The need to take and possess was so strong, everything else seemed insignificant in comparison.

"Yes, Nick, yes. Please."

Oh, god, that plea. She broke him with that plea.

He ran one hand up her spine, lifting her shirt as he

went so he could feel her soft, hot skin. So easy to rip the cotton away. So easy to take what she was offering.

But giving in wasn't an option. Not for him.

He forced his mouth from her and pulled back as far as he could—which wasn't very far. "Fuck me," he muttered.

"Yes, please," she said against his temple.

He couldn't help it; her comment made him laugh—a strained sound, but it broke some of the tension. He set his forehead against hers, closed his eyes, and sighed, forcing himself to move his hand out from under her shirt and his other up from her ass. That was the best he could do just then.

"This isn't going to work, Tatiana."

He nearly jumped out of his skin when she rubbed her palm over his cock through his jeans.

"I don't know," she murmured. "Seems to me everything is *working* just fine."

He groaned. "Tatiana, we can't." God, her hand on him. He needed her to stop stroking him, but he couldn't quite bring himself to move her. When he tugged her closer again, despite his intentions, without even realizing what he was doing, he cursed and stepped away. Still too close, but at least she wasn't touching him anymore.

"No," he said, narrowing his eyes.

She smiled and made to move toward him.

"No!" He pointed at the couch. "Sit. Stay."

She laughed and raised her brows. "I'm a cat, not a dog. I don't sit and stay."

"Damn it, just…stay in here. I'll be back in a few minutes."

He escaped upstairs before she could distract him again. His pulse pounded and her scent covered him. He couldn't think straight. He locked the bathroom door behind him, stripped off his clothes, and stepped into an icy shower.

Which did nothing to take the edge off.

Taking his erection in hand, he pumped his fist until his orgasm tore through him. The release was hollow and didn't do much to calm his need. But it was enough to give him some breathing room. He hung his head under the cold water and tried to wash away Tatiana's scent.

He'd ended up like this more often than he cared to admit over the years. His head full of her, his hand on his own cock. He turned to look at the locked door. He could still smell her, despite the water and soap. He shouldn't have brought her into his house. He'd have to move now.

Not that it would do him any good. The combination of her scent and his was going to haunt him for the rest of his life, pushing him that much closer to the insanity he'd always known lurked just beneath the surface.

He was, after all, his father's son.

He punched the water off and climbed out of the shower. Of all the Chernikov brothers, he was the most like their father—in looks and personality. It was only a matter of time before his father's weaknesses rose up to claim him as well. He should have known Tatiana would be the catalyst for his fall.

With a towel around his hips, he crossed the hall to his bedroom, locking that door as well. Tatiana was still downstairs, but he didn't trust himself not to call her up here to join him in bed. The lock wasn't so much to keep her out as to keep himself in.

By the time he finished dressing, he felt some semblance of control return.

Now he had to face her. And convince her to leave him to his isolation.

CHAPTER THREE

Tatiana listened to the shower shut off and the bathroom door open and close. Her body still hummed with need, and it was all she could do not to climb the stairs and make Nick pick up where they'd left off.

But he'd been right to stop. She wasn't even supposed to be with him outside the Run. Fucking him now would risk the very thing she was here to do. Oh, but she wanted him.

That kiss!

She'd never felt anything like that before, the desperation and heat, her body tightening and melting all at once. She'd had mild levels of lust with a few human men, but nothing like this. She could still breathe in their mingled scents and the combination was perfection. Tiger catnip. Somehow she had to convince him to join her next Run without actually jumping his bones beforehand.

As he came down the stairs, his hair still damp from his

shower, she had a hard time convincing her baser self that restraint was the best course of action. Her pulse thrummed the closer he got. She still felt the imprint of his palm against her bare skin. Her tiger growled and whispered, *more. Him.*

Yes.

He sat across the room from her, his mouth tight, his eyes hooded. He was brooding. She hated men who brooded. Or she thought she did. Nick carried it off with such intensity, she shivered. Everything the man did ticked all her boxes. He was nuts if he thought she'd walk away from that.

When he didn't say anything for several minutes, she gave in and started the conversation. "My next Run is in two weeks."

"I'm not going."

"I've got two weeks to convince you. After what just happened, don't try to tell me you don't want me."

"That doesn't matter. *We* can't happen."

"Why?"

"I'm too old for you."

She laughed. "Since when has age ever been a thing among our people?" He was fourteen years older than her, but since their kind lived between one hundred and twenty and one hundred and thirty years on average—and a few lived much longer—even his forty-two years was still young in the grand scheme of things. "That's not a good enough excuse. Try again."

"The others will fight me."

"It's not their say, Nick. It's mine. You're my choice. You just need to run."

"And what if I do? Then what?"

She frowned. "What do you mean?"

"Even if we spend this estrous together, chances of you getting pregnant are low. And unless you get pregnant, you'll just have to keep running."

"Then *we* keep running."

"In between, the others will attempt to…dissuade me."

She frowned. "Meaning?"

"They'll come after me. I've spent five years building a life here. A nice, quiet, peaceful life. I haven't had to fight other tigers in all that time. And I don't want to bring that kind of chaos down on this town. They've accepted me here. They don't deserve to have their home invaded by a group of angry tiger shifters."

"The others can't do that." She leaned forward. "You haven't been banned from the Run. You're allowed to compete for a mate. There is no fighting allowed."

"You think that'll matter?"

"Your grandmother is an elder. They have to follow the rules where you're concerned."

"And the unspoken rule for me and my brothers has always been that we were the bottom of the barrel and therefore subject to challenges and threats—everything short of killing us is acceptable. My grandmother isn't allowed to stop it. The only reason my father is still alive is because of the deal my grandmother made with the other elders. That deal meant she had to withdraw her official power and support from her grandsons."

"But…"

"No buts, Tatiana. This is how it is. And since I don't want my father executed for his crime, I've accepted the situation. Even tried to make the best of it."

Her heart hurt for him and his brothers. She knew their story—she'd made a point of learning everything she possibly could about Nick. She hadn't been brave enough to ask Elizaveta about her son Ivan's crimes, but she had admitted to the elder that she wanted Nick. Elizaveta had encouraged her interest.

With that kind of support, Tiana had been sure she'd be able to get Nick back to the Run. The damned man was a lot more stubborn than she'd counted on.

What she hadn't realized was that the other males might come after him despite the fact he was her choice. That wasn't supposed to happen. The whole point of the Mate Run was to eliminate fights and challenges between the males.

She shook her head. "They can't come after you to prevent you from running," she insisted. "I don't care what the unspoken rules for you and your brothers are. The rules of the Run are very clear. And you haven't been banned. You're allowed to participate."

"Don't be naïve."

She growled and launched off the couch. "Don't be condescending. The other males are not allowed to prevent any individual male from running."

"You think they'll announce that they came after me?"

"You gonna let other people tell you what to do with your life?"

"And what are you trying to do?"

She blinked. She'd expected him to get mad. She'd been goading him on purpose. Instead, he sat there calmly, just staring at her.

Damn him and his logic. He was twisting her reasonable arguments. She stalked the length of the room to burn off her frustration. When it didn't work, she spun on him and pointed. "I'm not trying to keep you from something you want. I'm trying to talk you into taking something I *know* you want. Something you can have." She straightened her shoulders. "And I'm not giving up just because you're afraid of a fight."

His eyes flared with a spark of anger. "I'm not afraid to fight. I've been fighting my entire life."

"Then fight now!"

"No."

"Why? And don't tell me it's because you don't want me or what I'm offering you. Don't even try to lie about that."

"Fine," he growled.

He stood in front of her in a blink. She gasped, startled by his sudden move.

"I am sick to death of fighting. I *like* the peace I have now. And there's nothing you can offer me that will be worth going back to the fight."

He may as well have hit her in the chest. The blow was so physical she actually took a stumbling step back from him. The swell of pain almost choked her, and she had to blink back tears.

His expression softened. "Tatiana…"

She raised a hand for silence. Staring at the floor, she took a few long, slow breaths, until the shock of pain passed, leaving only a dull ache in its wake.

Finally, she said, "I'm going to go back to the motel now because I have a few things to do, and we both need to cool off." She met his gaze again. "But this is not over. What we could have is worth fighting for, Nick. I'm going to convince you of it. I'm not leaving here until I do."

Before he could say anything else, she grabbed her coat and walked out the door. She didn't want to hear anymore just yet. She had to rally her emotions.

She knew deep inside he'd said what he had to hurt her and force her to give up. She knew he'd been mean on purpose, so she wasn't going to give him the satisfaction of allowing his comment to drive her away.

She meant what she'd said. What was between them, the potential of what they could have, was worth fighting for, and she'd convince him of that, no matter what it took.

CHAPTER FOUR

Nick stared at his front door for long minutes, disgusted with himself. She couldn't understand what life was like for him, what she would be getting into with him. But she hadn't deserved his cruelty.

He pushed his fingers through his hair and pulled hard until his scalp ached.

It was for her own good. He'd done that, said that, to drive her away for her own good.

The logic didn't prevent guilt from wrapping a tight hand around his throat.

He shook off the unwanted emotions and headed back to the diner. He had to get ready for the lunch rush. He didn't have time to hide in his house and brood.

He hated brooding anyway.

When he stepped back into the little diner, Jane was signing an invoice for a produce delivery. She looked up and raised her eyebrows at him. He shook his head and went directly to the kitchen.

A few minutes later she followed him. "Well?" she demanded, crossing her arms over her chest.

"Well, what?"

"Explanation, please."

"No."

"Nikolai Chernikov, we have been working together for five years. I helped you make this place a success. If that woman is here to drag you back into the big wide world, I deserve to know."

"What the hell makes you think that?" Nick frowned. Jane was entirely too perceptive.

"It's obvious she's someone significant to you. An ex-wife?"

"Never been married."

"Ex-girlfriend, then."

"No."

"Current girlfriend?"

"No."

"Someone else's wife who wants to fuck you?"

He scowled at her. "Jane, what the hell are you talking about?"

"I saw the way you two looked at each other. Thought the diner was gonna catch fire, there were so many sparks."

He turned his focus to cleaning the grill, avoiding her too-knowing gaze. "It's nothing. Don't worry. She'll be gone soon."

"Taking you with her?"

"No."

"Why?"

That made him look up. "You want me to leave?"

"Course not. We like having you here and you know it. You're one of us now. We don't give up our own easily. 'Specially after what you did for us with that gang of thugs."

"That was nothing."

"It wasn't nothing. They were terrorizing us. You got rid of them."

"You know I hate talking about it." When he'd arrived in Eirene, the townspeople were being plagued by a pack of werewolves they'd thought were a biker gang. Nick had paid off the alpha and established territorial boundaries that kept the werewolves out of Eirene. It hadn't been a big deal, but the people of Eirene kept making a fuss over it.

"Nick…" She trailed off and shrugged. "Anyway, none of us want you gone, but you're a young man."

He snorted at that.

"Younger than me," she pointed out.

Actually, he was older than Jane by six years. But his tiger shifter genes made his forty-two look more like he was barely thirty.

"You haven't taken up with any of the women here," Jane continued, "despite some interesting attempts to entice you. I find it hard to believe you want to spend the rest of your life celibate."

He didn't answer, just focused on scraping the grill.

"Beyond that being a waste of a good man," she said with a little smirk, "I want to see you happy."

"I am happy."

"Bullshit."

"Such language," he teased.

She shook her head. "Stubborn man. Fine, you want to keep your secrets, keep your secrets. But if you decide to leave us, I want to know ahead of time. I don't want to wake up one day to discover you've disappeared, and I'm out of a job."

"I'd never do that to you." He straightened and faced her. "I'm not going anywhere. I promise."

"Don't make those kinds of promises. They might come back to bite you in the ass."

She left him to his cleaning and his thoughts. Nick stared at the grill, frustration twisting his gut and his brain.

"Well, hell." He turned his attention back to his work and forced thoughts of Tatiana and the conversation with Jane away. He didn't want to think about this anymore. *Work, Nick*, he told himself. *Focus on work.*

The rest of it would just have to wait.

After taking care of a few work emails, Tiana spent the afternoon exploring the little town of Eirene. Nick had picked a lovely place to call home. The town was surrounded by thick pine woods and nestled against tall mountain slopes. The area was perfect for allowing him to stretch his tiger.

The town proper was a beautiful collection of quaint wood and stone buildings. Main Street was dotted with a combination of tourist shops and local businesses, like Nick's diner. The lamp posts, sidewalk trees, and the wires

stretched over the road were wrapped in silvery decora-
tions and little white lights for the winter holidays. She
imagined the street would be beautiful at night when all the
lights were flickering and the snow reflected back the
sparkles.

The air was crisp and clean. The noise from passing
cars was muted. Despite there being excellent skiing
throughout the area, the town didn't seem to be tourist
heavy, but it wasn't empty, either. There were plenty of
people on the sidewalks, going about their daily business,
and enough tourists to keep Eirene healthy and prosperous.

The place felt nice. Comfortable. Peaceful.

Easy to see why Nick had picked Eirene.

She wandered into a little antique shop and perused the
merchandise. The shop was half a block from Nick's diner
and almost without conscious thought, she moved toward
the large front windows to stare at the restaurant. It was
quiet at the moment, still a few hours away from dinner.
She could tell Nick was inside, as she easily sensed him at
this distance.

Despite her resolve, she wasn't sure what to do next.
How did you convince someone to love you? Especially
when they were determined not to.

The bell over the shop door rang and Tiana glanced
away from the diner long enough to see who'd entered.
Nick's waitress—Jane—stomped snow off her boots and
glanced around. When she spotted Tiana, she headed right
toward her.

Ah, hell. Tiana hadn't counted on having to deal with a
jealous human woman with her sights set on Nick. She

should have expected it. The man was gorgeous. Probably every woman in town wanted him.

"I'm Jane Emmerson," the woman introduced herself without preamble, extending her hand.

"Tatiana Loban-Gupta. Most people call me Tiana." The woman's handshake was firm but not aggressive.

"It's nice to meet you. What do you want with our Nick?"

Tiana raised her brows at the "our Nick". "I want to marry him," she said, returning the woman's bluntness.

"Does he want to marry you?"

Tiana pressed her lips together before answering. "I think so. But…he's got some baggage that's made him reluctant to get involved."

"Yeah, I know all about baggage." Jane motioned her away from the window, to a small table at the back of the shop. "You drink tea?"

Tiana nodded.

Jane motioned to the store's proprietress, a lovely older woman with short dark hair, porcelain skin, and a comfortably plump figure. "Two cups, please, Mindy?"

"Coming right up. Milk and sugar?"

"Yes for me," Jane said.

"Yes, please," Tiana echoed.

Once they were settled with two steaming cups of a rich Earl Grey in front of them, Jane leaned back in her seat and studied Tiana. Tiana didn't flinch or shy away from the scrutiny. She was busy sizing up the other woman herself.

"You intend to take Nick away?" Jane finally asked.

"If he wants to live here, we can live here. I like the town; what I've seen of it."

"What do you do for a living?"

"I'm a marketing consultant. I mostly work with small businesses looking to grow."

"Based out of a big company?"

"No. I work for myself."

"Does that mean you can live anywhere you like?"

"So long as I have an Internet connection and there's an airport within driving distance. Can I ask you something?"

Jane made a go-ahead motion with her hand.

"Why 'our' Nick? He's lived here…five years. This is a small town. Why would you accept a stranger into your midst so easily? What did he do for you?"

Jane smiled. The expression softened her otherwise world-weary face. Until that moment, her dark eyes were hard and unyielding. But now she looked…kind. And very pretty.

"We're all strangers here, you might say," she finally answered. She looked toward the front window. "You know the island of misfit toys? From that old Christmas cartoon?"

Tiana shook her head. She hadn't watched much TV as a kid and had never really developed the habit as an adult. Her family had always been more about spending time together doing things—camping, hiking, board games, travel, trips to museums, hunting. Her parents believed there was too much to do in life to spend a lot of time in front of a television.

Jane shrugged. "Well, you might not get the reference

then, but this town is a bit like that island. Lot of us came in broken. We found a home here."

"What broke you?" she asked quietly. Suddenly, the woman across from her seemed more vulnerable and Tiana's curiosity spiked. A town of broken people seemed exactly the kind of place Nick would settle.

Jane sipped her tea before answering. With a sigh, she said, "Oh, it's a clichéd tale. Bad man. Pregnant, single girl, too young to know what do to with herself. When I found out my son was on the Autism Spectrum, I got my shit together enough to leave his father. Didn't want my boy to take the beatings I was getting just because he couldn't communicate."

She set her cup down very carefully. "So I moved around a bit, taking odd jobs, trying to find ways to help Ben. Finally got in touch with a cousin in Kansas City who was a speech therapist. I was mostly just looking for suggestions, but she said if I could get to her, she'd work with Ben. I couldn't afford the therapies he needed otherwise, so I up and moved us. Again. On the way there, my old banger car crapped out on me just outside of town."

"And you haven't left since?"

She laughed. "No. I worked until I could afford to buy another cheap car, then continued on my way. I was pretty desperate for the help my cousin was offering. But by the time I'd made enough for the car, I'd gotten to know the people. I loved it here. Ben's needs took precedence, though. I got to Kansas City and my cousin started working with him immediately. We had to home school him initially, but eventually we got him into school. After four years, working my ass off to keep a roof over our heads, I saw huge improvement in my boy."

Her smile made Tiana's heart ache. So much love there.

Jane took a deep breath and refocused on Tiana. "All that time, I couldn't get this place out of my heart." She waved at the shop, but the gesture seemed to encompass the whole town.

"When did you come back?"

"Seven years ago. When my boy was ten and communicated at close to age level. He's real high functioning. The speech was our biggest issue. Once we could discuss moving, he got behind the idea. He…he had one good friend, but his friend had just moved a few months earlier —parents wanted to live closer to family. Ben was sad to lose his friend, and eager to make a change. He was ready to come back here. So was I."

She leaned back in her chair and that little soft smile came back. "He's so freaking smart, my Ben. He's off to college next year. I can't believe it's that time already."

Tiana watched Jane's motherly pride shine through, and it overwhelmed her. She really wanted to experience that love herself. Her own family had been so close, so full of love and laughter, and arguments and fights and fun. She wanted that same kind of closeness in her own family— with a husband and children and all the chaos. All the love.

She just had to convince Nick they could have that together.

Jane picked up her tea again. "So, that's my story. I was here about two years before Nick arrived, and I'd settled in like a local. When Nick rolled in, we recognized one of our own. He bought the diner from the previous owner, who wanted to retire, and he's been a fixture ever since."

"And that was that? You just took him in?"

"Yeah. Well, Nick did a bit more for us, too. But we would have accepted him no matter what. Like I said, we recognized a kindred spirit."

"What did he do for you?"

The bell over the door jingled and a young woman walked in with a toddler in tow. She waved at Jane and the shop's owner before moving toward one side of the shop where some old toys were shelved. The toddler squealed in delight. Tiana grinned at the little girl. When she looked back, Jane was watching the two with the same sort of fond expression she got when talking about the town.

"You really love it here, don't you?" she asked.

Jane raised her brows. "First home I've ever had. Best home I've ever had. These people are like family. And I'm protective of family." On the last sentence, her smile dropped away and she held Tiana's gaze.

"I'm protective of family, too. Believe me. I understand."

"You want kids?"

"More than I can tell you."

"They're hard. Every stage is tough."

"I know. I have six siblings, four younger than me."

"Not the same as having a kid of your own."

"Fair enough. I'm prepared for the tough."

"You're young."

Tiana smiled. "Not that young."

Tigers aged a little differently than humans and their

life spans were much longer. It wasn't unusual for humans to misjudge a tiger's age. At twenty-eight, she *was* young for both species, but not a girl who didn't understand how the world worked. As she held Jane's gaze, she realized Jane probably knew "how the world worked" at a much, much younger age. Suddenly, Tiana felt a pang of protectiveness for the woman, an urge to take away any pain she might have experienced. The incongruity of that would probably make Jane laugh.

"They are worth it," Jane said in a soft tone. "Kids. They'll break your heart in so many ways. But it's all worth it."

Tiana raised her mug in a toast. Jane followed suit. They sat quietly for a few minutes, drinking their tea.

Then Tiana said, "I don't want to take Nick away from the place he feels comfortable. I just want to share it with him."

Jane nodded. "Good. In that case, I won't warn him off you."

"You would have done that?"

Jane stood, leaving a few dollars on the table. "Of course. Why do you think I'm here?" She waved to the mother, toddler, and shop owner, all standing around the old toys now, then she turned toward the door. "Just don't break his heart," she said on her way out of the shop. "None of us will take kindly to that."

Tiana remained where she was for a bit longer, mulling over what Jane had told her.

Island of misfit toys.

That sounded…perfect.

CHAPTER FIVE

Nick knew the minute Tatiana walked into his diner. He'd felt her wandering around his town all afternoon, and it was all he could do not to go after her and drag her back to his house. Having a job to do, customers to make happy, helped. The diner was a lot of work. There was always something he had to do. But even that distraction wasn't enough to keep his thoughts off her.

He was the only one cooking tonight, so he didn't go out to her right away. Since he'd taken over the diner, the place was rarely quiet during meal times. Finding this town, this business, had been a blessing for him. And outside of that one early negotiation with the alpha of the local werewolf pack, he'd been able to live here quietly for all these years.

He was afraid to break that peace, terrified his mind would snap like his father's—just like all the other tigers thought—if he did anything to change the status quo.

Tatiana was asking him to risk that. She didn't know what she was courting by shaking up his world. He couldn't face driving her down the same hole his mother had fallen in to. If he let himself fall in love, he risked history repeating itself.

As he cooked and plated up each order, he reminded himself again and again, his caution was for Tatiana's own good. He'd just have to make her see that.

He looked through the order window and spotted her sitting at the counter. She smiled and waved, then went back to talking to the man sitting next to her. Charlie Sanchez was a town fixture; a man in his nineties, he'd actually been born in Eirene and always had plenty of stories to tell. When Charlie grinned at Nick, Nick narrowed his eyes in warning. There were some stories and rumors Nick didn't want Tatiana hearing second hand.

Charlie grinned around his dentures and faced Tatiana again, giving her a little wink.

Nick growled quietly and went back to cooking.

It was well past nine o'clock when he could finally leave the kitchen. He stepped into the dining room to see Tatiana sitting in a booth talking with two of his regular customers, with Jane standing over them laughing at whatever they were discussing. The two women in the booth spotted him before Tatiana and they scrambled up.

"So nice to meet you, Tiana," Rachel Maxwell said. She glanced at Nick and grinned before saying to Tatiana, "We'll talk more soon."

"Hi, Nick," the second woman, Betty Alonso, said as he

reached the table. "Don't worry, we'll settle the bill with Jane."

They practically dragged Jane to the register, leaving Nick alone with Tatiana.

"What did they tell you?" he asked, standing over her, trying to ignore the way her scent invaded his head and made him dizzy.

"We were just telling stories. No big deal." She gestured to the bench opposite her. "You've been working hard all night. Sit."

Reluctantly, he settled into the booth. "Did they manage to scare you off?"

"Opposite, actually." She chuckled at his scowl. "Don't worry, they only revealed the most embarrassing stories they know."

"What?" He started ticking through the options and his scowl deepened. They wouldn't actually tell her about that time Margery Bingham draped herself naked across his prep-table, would they?

She laughed and the sound sent a sharp shock of excitement down his spine. He clenched his hands under the table to keep from reaching for her. Damn the chemistry between them. He should *not* have this much trouble resisting a woman.

"Worried?" she said.

"No."

She stared at him, that half-smile hovering on her full lips. Finally, she said, "If I were you, I'd be more worried about what Charlie told me."

He raised his brows and waved a hand for her to continue.

Instead, she said, "You've picked a really lovely place to live, Nick. The people here are great. I've never been part of a small town before. To be honest, I didn't think I'd like having so many…people able to follow my life the way they can in a town this size." She hesitated over the word "people" and he knew she had been about to say humans. "But this place is unique."

"Yes, it is."

"Jane cornered me earlier today."

"Fuck." He ran a hand through his hair and glared at his head waitress. She raised her brows and stared back without flinching. "Fuck," he muttered again as he faced Tiana. "What did she say?"

"She wanted to know my intentions. It was pretty sweet, actually. Like a protective mother. Except you're older than she is. Does she know that?"

"No. What did you tell her?"

"That I wanted to marry you."

He blinked at her bluntness. This wasn't anything he didn't know. She wouldn't be here trying to force him back to the Run if she didn't want to keep him around. At least, he'd assumed as much, based on all her letters and emails.

But a part of him had thought this was just sex, just chemistry. She wanted kids and hadn't found another worthy tiger yet. She had gotten it into her head that he was worthy—a serious mistake on her part—but that didn't mean she wanted more than babies from him. To hear her say it aloud, that she'd declared to another person that she wanted to marry him was…

Tempting.

To cover his wavering emotions, he said, "I thought you were just looking for a good lay. And babies."

"That, too." Her smiled turned seductive. "You know we'd be good together, Nick. But I don't want a casual tiger father for my children. I want a partner. I want you."

"You don't even know me."

"Whose fault is that? I've been writing to you for months now. If you'd answered me even once, I might not have had to come here."

"My silence was my answer."

"It's the wrong one."

"Damn it, Tiana, I am not going to run. If I don't run, we have no option of having a relationship. Why make things worse by getting to know each other?"

She shook her head. "So fucking stubborn," she growled. "Okay, how about this? You spend the next few days getting to know me, and I'll get to know you. We'll… date. It's always possible we'll end up hating each other. Then you'll get your way. I'll leave."

He frowned, about to open his mouth when she interrupted.

"But you have to really give me a chance. You can't go all pouty and silent."

"Pouty?" His outrage made him straighten.

"Fine, tortured and silent." She smirked. "You have to seriously let me get to know who you are."

"What if who I am is tortured and silent?"

"I know better than that. I've been talking to the people coming in and out of this diner all evening. They adore you. People don't adopt and adore tortured, silent types who never give anything back. There's a reason they like you. You have to show me that."

"They like me because…" He trailed off and let out a breath. "Because I helped them with a problem after I arrived. They don't care if I'm tortured and silent now."

"I got hints of that. What problem?"

"Nothing. It's not an issue now."

She shook her head. "Nope. You have to tell me these things. That's part of the deal."

"I haven't made any deals yet."

She leaned back and crossed her arms over her chest. The move plumped up her already generous breasts and he couldn't seem to drag his gaze away from those soft mounds.

"Nick Chernikov, either we date for the next week and you let me get to know you, or I stick around and haunt your every move until you give in and run. Those are your choices."

With his gaze still focused on her breasts, he said, "Those are crappy choices." Feeling like a hormone-crazed teenager, he forced his gaze up and met her glare.

"Tough," she said.

Her bottom lip trembled a bit before she bit it to keep it still, and he knew he'd hurt her again. The sight made every soft, protective part of him want to pull her into his arms and hug away her hurt. He stayed where he was, his hands fisted against his thighs. But he couldn't bring himself to hurt her again.

"Fine. We'll…date. Although, if we get caught, it won't matter whether we end up liking each other or not. They'll officially ban me from the Run."

Those were the rules. Once a female started her Runs, the males had to stay away from her in between cycles. No dating, no courting, no attempts at currying favor outside the official Run. The rules were in place to make the Run feel like a fair contest between males. That fairness was an illusion, but it was an illusion that had kept their community from descending into chaos for the last two centuries. Hard to argue with that.

"No one knows I'm here," she said. "And I'm not going to tell anyone. Are you?"

He scowled. It would be a good way to get her to leave him alone. Being banned from the Run would eliminate any possibility of him trying for a tiger mate and would force Tiana to make another choice. He wouldn't be allowed to compete for her. She wouldn't be allowed to choose him.

For some reason, he couldn't force himself to pull that trigger.

"No, I won't tell anyone," he grunted.

"Then. Okay." She let her arms drop and took a shaky breath. "Good. So tomorrow night Jane tells me one of your other cooks is here and you have the night off. We'll have our first date then. You can pick me up at the motel."

"I'm not coming inside."

He'd let that comment slip out. He'd meant it to be an admonishment to himself. By the way her eyes narrowed and her lips curved up, he knew he'd revealed more than he'd intended.

"I'm not inviting you in," she said. "While we're dating, no sex."

"We're not supposed to have sex outside the Run anyway."

"Ha. We're not supposed to date either. But in this one thing, I'll stick to the rules. No sex."

He narrowed his gaze. Whether she meant to or not, she'd just issued him a challenge he was having a very hard time ignoring. His tiger wanted to rise to that challenge, to seduce her and take her and make her his mate. His tiger didn't give two fucks about Nick's desire for peace and quiet, not when such a deliciously tempting tigress was so close.

She rose, and he followed, still working to resist the call of his tiger.

"I'll see you at six tomorrow." She leaned in and kissed his cheek.

The soft brush of her lips against his skin set his blood pumping so fast he saw spots. Every nerve in his body lit up as her scent wrapped around him, invading him and sucking away his willpower. He flexed his fingers, so close to catching her in his arms he couldn't speak around the need.

She pulled back, smiled, and left him standing there, his body hot and tense and his soul more than a little desperate.

Dating. No sex. But chemistry that robbed him of speech.

What the hell had he just agreed to?

CHAPTER SIX

Tiana paced the small motel room as she waited on Nick. Part of her worried he might not show. She'd track him down and challenge him if he did stand her up, but the rebuff would hurt.

Fear lurked beneath her pacing. Fear that she would fail and the one man she wanted would refuse her. What would she do then? She simply didn't want any other tiger she'd ever met.

Before Nick, she'd been talking to Elizaveta about going to a Run in Russia. Maybe she'd have to go through with that. Meet other tigers. Run in completely different places. And hope.

The thought almost brought her to tears.

She sucked back the emotions because she didn't want Nick to show up and catch her being a sniveling, crying mess over something that hadn't even happened yet.

She checked her makeup in the tiny bathroom mirror to

avoid looking at the bedside clock again. "If he doesn't want you, Tiana, you will walk away," she told her reflection. "And, hey, you might find that despite the chemistry and everything you've learned about him, he's actually an asshole. You could hate him after tonight. Stop getting all worked up. You will be fine, even if this doesn't work."

She gave herself a sharp nod and returned to the bedroom. She hated this feeling of uncertainty and insecurity. A little part of her—the part that had worried something was truly wrong with her before she met Nick—was afraid that if things with Nick didn't work, she'd be destined to be alone for the rest of her life. That maybe something in her really was broken. She wanted to deny that sneaky, nasty little voice, but it was working with her insecurities to beat back her confidence. And she detested it.

"Fuck it," she growled.

She'd barely gotten the words out when a hard knock sounded on the door. Her stomach tumbled in crazy chaos as Nick's scent snuck into the small room. She'd been so preoccupied with worry, she hadn't even sensed him approach. Shaking off the mix of fear and excitement, she opened the door with a smile.

"What's wrong?" he asked before she could greet him.

"What?"

"You're upset. What's wrong?"

Her stomach did another crazy dance. She wasn't sure whether to be annoyed or overjoyed. She hadn't wanted him to know she was worried, but the fact that he looked so ready to leap to her aid made her heart thump faster.

This will work, she thought. *He wants me. We're compatible. We'll like each other. This will work.*

"Nothing's wrong," she said.

"You said 'fuck it'. Why?"

"How long have you been outside this door?" It couldn't have been long or she would have noticed. The fact that he'd managed to be there for any time at all without her knowing was disconcerting.

"Only long enough to hear you and you sounded upset. What's wrong?"

"Nothing. I promise. I was just talking to myself about…work." She lied blatantly, knowing he'd recognize it, that he'd be able to smell it.

His eyes narrowed, but he dropped the subject. At least for the moment. She couldn't explain to him what she'd been fretting about yet. That would have to come later, after things either worked out or they didn't.

They would, she told herself as she grabbed her purse and locked the motel door. This would work.

Nick gestured to the truck parked directly in front of her room. She crossed the sidewalk, passing in between the wooden planting boxes that separated the parking lot from the motel's first floor. The three-story motel sported rows of doors opening directly to the outside. There was no need to go through a lobby, which worked well for her. If she decided to let her tiger out for a walk in the woods behind the motel, she wouldn't have to call attention to herself when leaving her room.

They climbed into his four wheel drive, and she buckled up as he started the engine. "Where are we going?"

His scent filled the inside of the truck, overwhelming her, making her regret the "no sex" rule she'd put into place. He looked fabulous—dark jeans that fit him well, a button up white shirt under his heavy leather coat. His gorgeous eyes were greener in the limited light from the dashboard and his heavy-lidded look made her think of beds and tangled sheets. Her pulse kicked.

"There's a restaurant in Vail I've been wanting to try," he said. "It's a little bit of a drive. You good with that?"

"The drive is fine. And feeding me is always a good thing." She settled back into her seat. "I obviously like my food."

He cast her a slight frown. "Why obviously?"

With a gesture down the length of her body, she said, "You don't get curves like these without liking food." She laughed, but the sound dried up when she caught his expression as he looked over her curves.

He met her gaze for a split second before facing the road again, but that brief look was enough to spark Tiana's lust. Her skin tingled and tightened, her breathing sped up. Oh, but she could just crawl onto his lap right now and eat him up—speaking of hungers.

All her earlier worries got beaten to the back of her mind under the scent of desire painting the air around them. They had something. Something powerful. They could build on that.

This would work.

. . .

The restaurant was small and packed when they arrived, but the maître d' led them directly to a waiting table. The woman smiled a little come-on smile at Nick as she handed him a menu, then winked at Tiana as if they were sharing an inside joke. Tiana shook her head.

"How the hell are you still single?" she asked as she opened her menu. "I'm not saying I'm not grateful that you are. But really, even in that small town there have to be dozens of women trying to get in your pants." She knew for a fact there'd been more than a few, based on the stories she'd heard the night before.

He raised his brows at her comment. "I'm not sure how to respond to that."

"Don't worry, I'm not judging you or anything. I'm just…baffled."

"I'm too busy," he grunted and held up his menu.

Interesting answer. He was sex on a stick, but he was avoiding relationships. The women from the diner had confirmed he'd been single the entire five years he'd lived in Eirene—despite some pretty creative attempts to change his mind. The woman who'd draped herself naked across his workspace in the diner was a particularly colorful attempt.

There was nothing wrong with him physically. That had been obvious yesterday in his house. So, what was it?

"Do you not like human women?" she asked quietly. The room was noisy so she was pretty sure they wouldn't be overheard, but she still pitched her voice so only another tiger would hear her.

He frowned. "I like human women. I like women just fine."

"Yes, I got that impression." She set the menu aside. "So what is it, Nick? Why have you turned into a monk?"

"I'm not a monk," he said. Then shook his head. "I'm single because I don't want a relationship. And I don't date in Eirene because it's too small a town for casual flings."

"So. You leave town to get laid, then."

His cheeks actually colored and Tiana grinned. He was charming in his embarrassment. She wanted to push him a little more but decided she'd better give him a break—first date and all.

"What are you going to order?" she asked instead.

He rolled his shoulders as if loosening tight muscles and went happily into a discussion of the food choices. Listening to him talk about food was another kind of seduction. He was passionate about flavors and interesting combinations. His restaurant was mostly straightforward diner food, but he admitted to occasionally adding something a little more adventurous to his offerings.

"I could only convince a few dozen people to try the black chicken on squid ink pasta," he said with a little laugh. "They all loved it, but it wasn't on the menu for long."

She wrinkled her nose. "I've never even heard of black chicken before."

"It's ugly, but it tastes good. Like chicken."

"And I thought I was an adventurous eater. Well, except for eggs. Anything to do with eggs…" She shivered. Her tiger actually balked. When it came to food that only ever happened with eggs.

"Tell me about your job," he said as their first course was served. "I feel like I've been doing all the talking."

"I like listening to you discuss food." She took a sip of her fennel apple soup and rolled her eyes. "Oh, that's good. The hazelnuts are a wonderful addition."

He nodded. "My scallop is cooked perfectly, too." He looked around. "I can see why this place is so hard to get into."

"How'd you get a reservation last minute, then?"

He shrugged. "I know the head chief." His smile held a touch of something like pride. "She started out as a line cook at my diner."

Tiana blinked. "The person who made this used to work for you?"

"She's fantastic, isn't she?"

"Wow. How'd she learn to cook like this? And if she can cook like this, why did she work in your diner? No offense, but her menu is full of…serious cuisine. Like French culinary school stuff."

He laughed. "Believe it or not, she was a naturally superb home cook who didn't think she had the chops to own her own place. She came to work for me after her husband lost his job, and they were desperate for money. It took exactly one dinner service for me to recognize what I had in her. And that I wouldn't be able to keep her for long."

"How'd she get the money for this restaurant?"

His cheeks colored again and Tiana found herself

leaning a little closer, her elbows on the table as she studied him.

"I gave her a loan to get started. She paid me back last year."

"Why?"

He frowned. "Why, what?"

"Why did you give her a loan?"

"I… She wanted a restaurant and didn't have the credit for a bank loan. She was good enough to be really success-ful. It was a smart investment."

Tiana nodded. "Right. That's why you did it."

"You changed the subject. We're supposed to be talking about your job now."

"Fine." She smiled. "But you can't hide the fact that you're a good guy from me, Nick Chernikov. You've just given yourself away."

He rolled his eyes and turned back to his plate.

She regaled him with the details of her job after that. She was supremely proud of the work she'd done recently with two small charity businesses, raising their profiles and helping to increase their annual donations. She blushed and preened at the same time when he complimented her efforts.

As dinner progressed, the conversation flowed from work to books, books to movies, movies to skiing—he liked it, she'd fallen a lot the only time she'd tried—and from skiing to travel. They'd moved into discussions of places they'd each visited when she recognized how care-fully he was avoiding the topic of family, his or hers. They didn't talk about their people and the political and biological issues plaguing the tigers. They didn't talk about anything too serious.

By the time dessert arrived—a delicious concoction of chocolate and surprising chili spices—Tiana knew her worst fears were pointless. Nick wasn't an asshole. He was everything she'd hoped he'd be: kind, passionate about his work, loyal to those around him. Everything he showed her of his personality meshed with the stories the townspeople had spent last night telling her. He was honest, strong, a little too serious, but when he laughed it was breath-stealing. Smart and stubborn in equal measure.

And despite their limited time together, she knew her heart was his.

There wouldn't be any running in Russia after this. There couldn't ever be another man for her. She was done. Completely, head-over-heels in love. If Nick didn't come back to the Run now...

She'd just have to face her future alone.

CHAPTER SEVEN

By the time they got back to her motel, Tiana was about ready to toss her "no sex" rule into the dumpster. Her hands actually shook with need and lust. When Nick opened the car door for her, she tumbled out into his arms. She couldn't help it. Every nerve in her body screamed for contact, touch, the rub of bare skin against skin.

He didn't release her immediately, as she'd half expected. In fact, he tightened his hold so she was pressed against the full length of him. His gaze moved over her face and zeroed in on her lips. She tingled under the intensity of his look.

"You said 'no sex'," he reminded her in a voice deep and rough.

"Yeah, well, I meant it at the time."

"Now?"

"Still mean it. Just don't like it." She leaned in and kissed him because she couldn't resist.

A goodnight kiss was how a first date was supposed to end, right? This was just part of the night. Not pushing her resistance too far. Not breaking more rules than they could recover from.

As soon as her lips parted, the instant his tongue swept into her mouth and their kiss turned serious, all thoughts of rules went out of her head. She ground her hips against his and moaned when his hands moved to her ass to hold her close. His cock was a hard, thick line against her abdomen, a temptation that begged for her attention.

She ran her hands over his back and down to his ass, squeezing tightly. His groan sent sparks of excitement racing over her. She dragged her mouth from his to kiss his neck and take in more of his scent. He was the most delicious thing she'd tasted all night, and that was saying something after that dinner.

He moved one hand to her breast while his other stayed around her waist, keeping her pressed tight to him. She hadn't closed her coat, so he had as much access as her blouse and bra allowed, but oh, how she wanted to feel his hand on her bare skin. He rubbed his thumb over her nipple until it was a hard little peak against her clothing. Her imagination filled with thoughts of his mouth on her nipple and she shivered, rubbing harder against him.

When he took her mouth again, she dove into the kiss with an eagerness that might have embarrassed her with any other man. With Nick this felt so natural, so electric that she could only feel her need.

She wanted him so much she didn't care that they were in a parking lot. She barely considered that they might have an audience. She simply didn't care. She wanted to unzip his pants, push her own trousers out of the way, and take him right there, standing against his truck.

But the idea that there was a bed just a few steps away struck her as much better. Could she resist him long enough to get the door unlocked? If not, she'd pay for the repairs from breaking the doorframe.

When she pushed him back, intending to pull him to the room, he surprised her by dropping his hold and taking a step back to put space between them.

"Goodnight," he grunted, then hurried to the driver's side of the truck.

She barely had time to close her door before he backed out and skidded away, leaving her standing in the parking lot staring after his taillights, her pulse pounding, her breathing erratic, her body on fire.

What the hell?

She was inside the room before she realized what had happened.

She'd told him she meant it when she'd said no sex yet. He probably thought she'd been pushing him away rather than trying to steer him to her room.

The realization made her laugh. A shaky, breathy, self-deprecating laugh, but still a laugh. He'd respected her wishes, despite the power of that kiss, despite her own lack of willpower. He was abiding by the rules she set.

Rules that would allow him to run for her.

Hope and fear warred equally in her gut as she went to

the bathroom to change for bed. He wanted her, and a part of him was keeping the option of the Mate Run open. But there was a lot left unsaid between them…especially about family, and why he had given up on the Run. His family history was complicated. She knew the stories, but there was something more there holding him back.

As she washed her face, she considered the possibilities. Until they talked about it, though, she'd only be guessing.

He wanted her. That was a good start. He liked her enough to respect the rules she'd put in place for their "dating", which encouraged her more. But the shadow hanging between them worried her.

She stripped off her trousers and blouse, and then stared out the high bathroom window. She was too restless and edgy to sleep. The motel backed up to the woods. She could use a run. Her tiger needed to get out to release some of this excess energy. She needed to clear her head, so full of lust and Nick's scent. Then she'd be able to think, to plan. To find a way to overcome Nick's resistance.

Yes, a run would be just the thing.

B y noon the next day, when Nick hadn't seen or felt any sign of Tiana, he started to worry.

At first, he'd been grateful. It had taken every ounce of self-control left in him to walk away from her last night—run away, more like. He wasn't sure he had enough control left to resist her anymore, and he'd been deathly afraid that if she walked into his diner for breakfast, he'd drag her back to his place and fuck her until the world ended, no matter what rules she'd set.

His body hadn't stopped throbbing with need since he'd driven away from her. Nothing helped, nothing stopped the ache. She was so far under his skin now, he had to admit he'd lost this fight.

He *liked* her. He'd known he would. His tiger had been telling him for six years she was his. Her letters, her emails, assured him she was the kind of woman he'd fall for. He'd gone home last night and re-read everything, confirming all his worst fears. Their evening together had sealed the deal. She was…

She was worth running for.

Which made his situation that much worse. The more he wanted her, the more he liked her, the more desperate he was to keep her away from him and the darkness lurking beneath the surface.

When he made it through the breakfast rush without having to face her, he'd been relieved. He needed the space, the time, to get his emotions under control. But by the time the lunch rush started and he still hadn't even sensed her, a niggling worm of anxiety started to crawl through his gut.

She wasn't at the motel. The place was just beyond Nick's ability to feel her, but he'd not-so-casually asked one of his customers who worked the motel's front desk. The man hadn't seen her all morning, but the maid had been in to clean the room and it was empty.

So, she wasn't at the motel. And she wasn't anywhere in town—he'd definitely feel her here. A few people even asked *him* where she was, which meant no one else had seen her all morning either.

Worry dug a hole in his gut and sent him pacing the kitchen. Finally, after he'd burnt a second order of fries, Jane called in one of the other cooks.

"You need to go find her," she ordered. "I'm sure she's just fine. She probably went sightseeing in Vail or drove down to Denver for the day—"

"She would have told me if she was doing that," he interrupted.

"Fine. Still, I'm sure there's nothing to worry about, but you're going to burn the diner down fretting about her. So go. Get out of here. We can finish the lunch service."

Nick couldn't even find an argument in him.

He went back to his house first to get his truck, intent on driving to the motel first to get her scent, then following that as best he could. He wasn't a Tracker, but one of the greatest tiger Trackers in recent memory was the closest thing he had to a big sister, and he'd learned a few things from Alexis.

He was so focused on forming a search plan, he almost missed the note under his windshield wiper. Frowning, he snatched it up and opened the lined notebook sheet. The message made his blood run cold.

We have your woman. You want to see her alive again, meet us in the woods. You know the place. Come in human form or she'll suffer. ~Corwin

The werewolves had Tiana.

CHAPTER EIGHT

Nick could barely control his tiger by the time he reached the meeting place in the middle of pack territory, deep in the woods where no human would disturb them, in a clearing where the snow was light and the frozen ground peeked through the white.

He arrived in human form as the message demanded, but his skin itched with the need to shift and rend the threat to Tiana into bits. The darkness he'd always known he possessed rose up to edge his vision.

He held his control for her sake. He had to get her out of the wolves' territory unharmed. Nothing else mattered.

As soon as he entered the clearing, members of the local pack surrounded him. There were about twenty werewolves in all, most in human form. Two or three were already in wolf form. He ignored them all. He could feel Tiana. Her scent mixed with the musky smell of two wolves. She was being held in the woods, out of sight, but nearby.

He studied the currents and textures of her essence, so familiar now, searching out her mood. He'd expected to pick up the sharp acrid stench of fear or anxiety in her scent. Instead, all he caught was a strong punch of anger, like the smell of a raging forest fire.

He smiled, and his tiger stopped pushing him so hard to rip the pack to pieces.

His expression made the surrounding wolves bristle and a few growls filled the clearing. His smile grew.

Finally, their alpha made a dramatic entrance, appearing in the clearing with a burst of speed that might have intimidated a non-shifter. Nick remained impassive.

"Chernikov," the man greeted.

Chris Corwin was tall, lean, and had a hungry look to his sharp, angular features. Nick had never trusted the alpha, but they'd managed to hold the peace for years. In that time, Corwin had grown more desperate looking, the gleam in his eyes brighter. He wasn't crazy—there was nothing like that in his scent—but he wasn't a good man. He had a mean streak, a bully's personality that had rubbed Nick the wrong way in their one and only confrontation.

"You have something that doesn't belong to you," Nick said, not bothering with pleasantries.

"But she's so pretty. I like pretty things."

Nick heard Tiana growl and almost smiled again. Her anger did more to calm his rage than anything else. If she wasn't worried about her own safety, he could maintain his control and get them out of here without anyone getting hurt.

"We've got no problem with you, Corwin," Nick said. "I thought we had an understanding."

"We did. She invaded our territory. She's tiger. Therefore, she's broken the rules of our *understanding*."

Nick kept his expression neutral, but cursed inwardly. Sonofabitch. He should have warned her. He hadn't thought, hadn't been able to think since she'd arrived in town. He'd been assuming the werewolves had come into his territory or gone into neutral territory to get her. Corwin was a greedy bastard. When Nick got their note, he'd thought the wolves were using Tiana to shake him down.

He'd completely forgotten that she might want to run and that her run might take her into dangerous places. He'd been avoiding telling her about his dealings with the werewolves. The story left him…edgy and a little embarrassed, because of the way the people of Eirene had acted after.

Stupid mistake, not telling her. A mistake he'd be kicking himself for for years.

"My fault," he said to the alpha. "I forgot to tell her about the territory boundaries. Won't happen again. Let her go, and we'll get out of your hair."

"No, no, no. Not that easy." Corwin's voice carried through the trees.

Nick snarled. He really hated Corwin. He was mean and petty. According to all the rumors, the pack was in bad shape under his leadership. They'd been so desperate for money five years ago, they'd gone along with his plans to harass and threaten the people of Eirene. Most werewolves were like Nick's own people—they kept to themselves and avoided confrontations with humans. Going after a town the way this pack had was a sign of dysfunction and risked a backlash that could have gotten them wiped out.

Nick had come to town, discovered the problem, and solved it with a payoff. He had plenty of money—his father had signed everything over to him and his brothers when he'd left for South America. The wolves were in such bad straits, and Nick had been able to make a deal with Corwin that avoided a fight.

The town and its immediate surroundings were Nick's territory. Some of the woods opposite the pack's lands were also part of Nick's territory—so he had room to run. The pack kept everything else, and Nick promised never to enter their lands. In the fine print, he'd agreed to keep other tigers out, too, but he hadn't expected anyone other than his brothers to ever come to this area. It was traditionally wolf land and the tigers kept to themselves, avoiding dealing with other shifters as much as possible.

Unfortunately, Tiana had had Nick so wound up since her arrival, he hadn't considered the wolves as a possible threat.

He'd pay for that mistake now.

"Okay, Corwin, how much will it cost me this time?"

Nick had never been sure if the alpha had told his pack the details of the deal he'd made with Nick—or that the deal involved money rather than a challenge fight. But he didn't have time to worry about the alpha's machinations. Tiana was in those trees and she needed him.

Corwin's smile didn't drop but his eyes narrowed. "No money will pay for this breach, Chernikov."

"What do you want, then?" Nick worked hard to control his rising temper. "You wouldn't have left a note for me if you didn't want something."

The alpha flicked his wrist and two wolves stomped into the clearing with a glaring Tiana between them. She moved without having to be dragged, but her gaze was dangerously narrowed and her nostrils flared. Nick could practically see her tiger in the faint yellow glow of her eyes.

To his dismay, she was naked. She'd obviously been out running in tiger form when the wolves caught her. With any other tiger, he'd have barely noticed her nudity. But with Tiana, the sight of her beautiful, lush body made his head spin. She was the most gorgeous thing he'd ever seen.

His tiger rose again, ready to rip the wolves holding her apart just to get to her. A whisper rose in the back of his mind. *Mate. Mine.*

He ignored that worrying instinct, even as the dark rage edged his vision again.

"You okay?" he asked when she stopped glaring at the wolves to look him.

"I'm fine. You?"

"Be better when you're out of here."

She snorted. "Don't worry about me. I'm not." She growled at the wolf to her right, and the man actually took a step back before he crowded close to her again, gripping her arm tighter.

One of the women in the pack laughed at the man,

which made his expression darken. That wasn't good. If the wolf thought his status in the pack had just taken a hit, he might take out his embarrassment on Tiana.

Tiana stared at the laughing woman. When she met Tiana's gaze, she stopped laughing but she smirked.

"Come on, pretty," the wolf said. "I'll take you on."

Tiana looked the woman over and snorted, turning away with a dismissive head shake. The wolf growled but Tiana ignored her.

Damn, but Tiana was courting danger. In a fight, one tiger against one wolf, the tiger was likely to win. But they were two tigers surrounded by an entire werewolf pack. That didn't put the odds in their favor.

"Well, this is fun," the alpha said. "I'm tempted to let Rina have at your pretty tiger. But I think my boys would like her first."

"Not gonna happen," he and Tiana said at the same time.

He glanced at her and raised his brows. She grinned. The look shot right to his gut, skimming dangerously close to his heart on the way past.

"We'll pay a fine for the territory breach," Nick said. "But that's it. Then we're gone."

"I already said money wouldn't do it this time, Chernikov," the alpha growled. "We wolves fight over territory."

Nick sighed. Damn it. He'd been able to steer clear of fights since moving to Colorado. Now, because he'd been too distracted to warn Tiana about the wolves, he'd walked into the very thing he'd been avoiding.

He put his hands on his hips and hung his head, disgusted with his own stupidity. When he looked up, the alpha was smirking.

"Animal or human shape?" Nick asked without preamble.

"Me animal. You human."

"That's not a fair fight," Tiana snarled. "Coward."

The alpha glared at her. "Careful, pretty, or I'll turn my wolves loose on you while I'm eating your boyfriend's entrails."

Tiana's growl filled the clearing, a sound no human throat could produce. Nick's heart thumped hard, a combination of fear for her and pride in her strength. He should have known his Tiana wouldn't be cowed by threats.

Nick raised his brows at the alpha. "Well…are you going to shift, or keep posturing?"

The alpha glowered as he stripped off his shirt. He started his shift, his body convulsing and stretching. The sounds of bones cracking and rearranging, tendons popping and skin splitting filled the clearing. Hair ran along the man's arms, chest and legs. He hadn't bothered removing his pants, which meant the material got shredded.

Nick shook his head at the waste. This alpha had always struck Nick as rash. He'd never been sure why the pack kept him. From what he could smell, Nick was pretty sure at least two or three of the other wolves at the edge of the clearing were stronger than Corwin—there was a scent to power in shifters, a flavor Nick had trouble describing with words. But in the really powerful shifters, no matter the species, that scent had always reminded Nick of something dangerously hot, like ghost chilies. Corwin didn't have that in his scent, while some others in his pack did. Why didn't someone else take over?

Nick let the issue go. He didn't give a fuck about wolf politics. All he cared about was getting Tiana out of these woods safely.

While Nick waited on the alpha's shift—which wasn't very fast for a pack leader—he stripped off his own coat and shirt. The less he had in the way, the better. The frozen air bit into his skin, despite his naturally high body heat. He glanced at Tiana's naked body again.

She had on oversized boots to keep her feet from the frozen ground—not absolutely necessary for a tiger shifter, but he was glad to see it as the cold would still seep in through the strong, thick soles of her feet if she had to stand still too long. Other than that concession, she had no other protection from the winter weather. Her high metabolism would keep her from freezing while in human form, but she'd still catch a chill if she wasn't allowed to move. He gently tossed her his jacket.

She snatched it out of the air, a move that forced one of the wolves to scramble to regain a hold on her arm. She gave both men a look, and they let her go long enough for her to slip into the fleece lined coat. She wrapped it close and breathed in deeply. Nick knew she was taking in his scent. He got entirely too much satisfaction from her reflex.

When she smiled at him, his muscles tensed. Before he could react, the wolves grabbed her arms again and pulled her back toward the trees.

Nick glanced around and realized the clearing had

opened up. All the wolves had moved back to just inside the tree line. He faced the alpha, taking the man's measure now that he was in wolf form. He was huge—no one could ever confuse a werewolf for a real wolf. Tiger shifters had the advantage there as they blended in well with their non-shifter animal counterparts. Even a large werewolf was smaller than most tigers, but Nick had learned that size wasn't the mark of a dangerous predator.

The wolf paced in a tight back-and-forth line, sizing up Nick. Nick waited, watching, in no hurry to give away his own tactics. Fighting an animal while still in human form was tricky—and rarely done in the shifter world. Fighting an alpha wolf with something to prove was downright dangerous. Nick studied the wolf's movements, assessing his strength and muscle density, looking for vulnerabilities.

There weren't any obvious ones.

The wolf howled, setting the entire pack to howling. Nick winced. His sensitive ears ached from the assault of the discordant notes filtering through the pack's combined song. They weren't in sync. Another sign the alpha wasn't a good leader.

Since that was wolf business and nothing to do with him, he pushed it to the back of his mind and focused on Corwin, who'd resumed pacing.

Without any sign or warning, Corwin launched at him, mouth open, claws forward, moving faster than any ordinary wolf. Had he been human, Nick would have had his throat ripped out before he realized the alpha had even moved. But Nick was no human.

He tracked the wolf's flight and stepped aside at the

very last second, a move that sent the animal barreling into a tree. He was up and lunging at Nick again instantly, his growls vicious.

Nick took the second lunge, grabbing the wolf by the neck and back leg to fling him bodily into the trees. The animal crashed into two of his pack in a chaotic mess. Nick rolled his shoulders. Damned animal was heavy, but not as long as a tiger, so Nick had grabbed him wrong. He was used to fighting his own kind.

He reset his stance just as the alpha clawed back to his feet and charged again. This time, Nick took the full brunt of Corwin's weight and rolled with it, falling to his back and flinging the wolf over his head as Corwin's front claws raked over his chest. He rolled to his feet before the wolf landed and faced the animal again.

A trickle of blood rolled down Nick's chest. He ignored it.

As the alpha attacked again and again, Nick focused on throwing him, keeping him off balance, winding him when he could. Without claws and teeth, Nick couldn't win this fight by simply overpowering the alpha and taking his throat in his mouth. The only way to win was to wear Corwin out and either make him give up or knock him unconscious.

Unfortunately, the animal had a thick fucking skull and he just kept coming.

Nick grunted with the effort of throwing him *again* and forced down the sting of the cuts and slices he was taking. Around them, the wolves barked and howled. From the corner of his eye, Nick noticed either three more had shifted to wolf form, or more wolves were joining the entertainment. Though he focused on his opponent, some of the taunts and jeers from the onlookers reached him. A few were directed toward Nick, as he would have expected.

But louder voices were jeering at Corwin.

Ah, hell. That wasn't good.

CHAPTER NINE

Tiana's stomach lurched when Nick avoided yet another lunge from the increasingly erratic alpha. Nick was amazing. Most tigers couldn't fight as effectively in human form as they could in tiger form—especially against an animal. But Nick handled the wolf with a practiced touch.

Watching him fight drove home just how much fighting he'd had to do over the years. The thought made her heart ache for the young boy, learning how to take a beating and defend himself the hard way.

The wolf dove at Nick's side, catching him with a claw swipe that stopped Tiana's breath. Nick spun away at the last instant, turning what could have been a serious injury into a glancing scrape. Nick was accumulating a number of cuts and gouges, but they were superficial and healing quickly. The earliest ones weren't even visible anymore. Still, all those little wounds would eventually build up, take their toll, and maybe slow Nick down. He couldn't hurt the wolf in the same way while in human form, but he was making the alpha do most of the work, a steady slog to wear Corwin out.

From what she could tell, Nick was trying not to kill the alpha, just tossing him around until he either gave up or was knocked out. Unfortunately, as the surrounding wolves started to call and whistle at the combatants, the alpha's energy seemed to increase. As she'd expect, some of those taunts were directed at Nick, but a discordant note gained ground as the fight continued, insults directed at the alpha.

Oh, no. She'd seen enough of him over the long night to know he was arrogant, proud, and insecure in his position. Those were very dangerous traits. Having members of his pack call him weak in front of strangers would corner him, make him desperate to beat Nick.

And while Nick wasn't trying to kill Corwin, she wasn't sure Corwin would stop short of killing Nick.

She tugged at the two wolves holding her as they shouted support and encouragement to their leader, but they held tightly. Irritation at the confinement warred with her worry for Nick. She almost screamed when the alpha dove low and snapped his heavy jaws inches from Nick's hamstring.

Nick avoided the blow but was off balance when the alpha attacked again. This time, Nick took the weight of the animal and fell awkwardly against a tree. Desperate to help, Tiana jerked at the hands holding her again. They gripped tighter, but because of Nick's thick coat, she had wiggle room.

Nick threw the alpha bodily across the clearing, a feat that awed her, but she could tell the move cost him. He pushed off the tree slower than he'd been moving before and his shoulders sagged for an instant as he braced for another attack.

This wasn't fair. If Corwin was any kind of leader, he'd have challenged Nick fairly, both of them in animal form.

To her surprise, she heard those same thoughts in some of the jeers.

"Let him go tiger!"

"This is boring! Face the beast."

"Come on, Chernikov, show us your animal!"

Tiana took her eyes from the fight long enough to study the pack. A few of the ones who'd been in human form were changing to wolf, and those already in wolf form were edging closer to the fight.

She had an awful moment of certainty—they were going to help their alpha; they were going to gang up on Nick while he was still in his weaker form.

Rage rushed through her, making her tiger roar in her head. How dare they? This was already an unfair, unnecessary fight. No matter how good Nick was, he'd be in trouble facing half a wolf pack while he was still in human form.

Well, she had no intention of allowing it. She tested the men holding her arms again. Their grips were firm but not tight. If she was careful, she'd be able to slip from the coat and get some distance. She needed enough time to shift, and she wasn't sure how she was going to get that before Nick got hurt, but she had to try.

The men loosened their holds at the exact moment their alpha barreled into Nick again, and Tiana took advantage of their lapse. She slid free of the coat and her captors in a single move. One of the men scrambled to grab her again but missed as she jerked away. The other caught her more firmly, and pulled her back against his chest.

"Where you going, pretty?" he hissed in her ear. "We're not nearly done with you yet." He reached up and squeezed her breast in a bruising grip.

Outrage and disgust had her reacting on instinct. She reached back and grabbed his balls, twisting with her tiger strength until he squealed and dropped his hold. She spun and punched him in the throat before he could recover, a move which dropped him to a wheezing heap at her feet. The second guard dove for her and she swung back, taking him down with the kick she'd been practicing with her self-defense instructor, Alexis Tarasova. The move broke his knee with a satisfying crunch. His scream was barely audible over the rising noise from the rest of the pack—howls and shouts, cheers and taunts filling the air.

She looked back to the fight in time to see the alpha spin and launch at Nick while Nick was still adjusting his stance after having tossed off a second wolf. This time, Nick wasn't fast enough and the alpha's massive mouth closed over Nick's arm. Even at a distance, Tiana heard the bone crack.

"No!" she roared, the sound pure animal. All her fear, anger and rage poured into her shift as she let her tiger out, changing forms faster than she was normally able.

When she blinked with tiger eyes and took in her

surroundings, another two wolves were charging toward Nick while the alpha rose slowly from a heap at the base of a tree, blood dripping from one of his eyes. She roared again, the sound cutting through the other noise, and rushed at the two wolves.

They were so surprised to face an angry tiger that neither was ready to defend himself against her. With her teeth, she grabbed one up by the scruff and tossed him back into the crowd. The second recovered enough sense to attack, but she was so angry, she rose on her hind legs, took him with her forepaws and slammed him into the ground. When she stepped on his throat, he stilled beneath her, whining.

She wasn't here to kill anyone—and to be honest, she wasn't sure if she could since she'd only ever killed food before—but they didn't need to know that. She backed off and growled low, lifting her lips in a snarl that showed teeth. The wolf under her scrambled back to the safety of the pack, limping.

She turned toward the fight in time to see Nick whirling at speeds almost too fast for her to see. He was attacking now, charging the alpha, picking him up and slamming him into trees again and again—one handed. He was wild, vicious… magnificent.

When she felt movement from behind, she spun to face the wolves and snarled. They held back, though it was clear some of them were chaffing to reach their alpha.

She kept half her focus on the pack, the other half on Nick so she could jump to his aid if he needed her.

He didn't need her.

As she watched, Nick pulled Corwin into a choke hold, ignoring his claws as the wolf fought to breathe. The scent of blood filled her nostrils, instinct making her growl and chuff. Nick's blood. But not enough to be dangerous. The alpha's struggles weakened, his big body went limp, and his eyes rolled back. Nick held him two more beats, then tossed him aside.

He whirled to face the rest of the pack, circling to glare at each of them. She left her post and eased up to him, nudging his leg with her shoulder. Without looking down at her, he settled a hand on the back of her head, his touch protective and gentle.

"Anyone else want a go?" he shouted, his voice harsh and guttural. His tiger was right there, ready to come out.

Because his arm was still limp and useless, she didn't want him to shift yet—it would complicate the bone resetting and might force her to break the bone again to get it to heal correctly. She settled closer to him, her shoulder pressed against his leg, letting him know she was here to support him.

The wolves surrounding them shuffled uncomfortably and exchanged looks she couldn't read.

"Are we done here, then?" Nick said into the awkward silence. "Idiot pride and territoriality satisfied?" No one answered. Not a single wolf stepped forward to take the lead. "Where the hell is your beta?" Nick snarled, his voice settling to his more normal octave now.

More shuffling, more looks, more unease. A scent rose to tangle with the pack's already musty canine smell, a complicated mix of flavors that her tiger nose interpreted as fear and disgust.

Finally, one of the men stepped forward. He was taller than the alpha, with dark hair and blue eyes. He was the wolf who'd given her boots to wear when they'd left the pack's cabin to meet Nick. She thought she'd heard someone call him Adam.

As they'd held her captive through the night, she'd scented the essence of a few wolves she thought might be stronger than the current alpha. This particular wolf was one of them. Another looked a lot like him and she'd guessed from their scent signatures they were related. Knowing there were wolves stronger than the alpha had worried her more than being held by the group, because it hinted at a dysfunctional pack. And a dysfunctional were-wolf pack was a dangerous thing.

Given what Nick had implied—that he'd paid the alpha off before this—and the surprise she'd smelled at that comment, she suspected things weren't getting better soon.

The man who'd stepped forward looked Nick in the eyes when he spoke. "No beta in our pack. He doesn't like them." He nodded to the fallen leader. "He's going to be pissed when he wakes up."

"If he comes into my territory looking for trouble, I won't stop at just knocking him out. The breach in your territory was an accident. I have no quarrel with your pack. But I will defend my town if you come looking for me."

"No interest in your town. No interest in you." He glanced at the downed leader again. "We have some pack business to take care of, anyway. Get your woman out of here."

Tiana snarled, her ruff rising in irritation, a threat in her tone. Nick stroked his hand down the back of her head, settling her fur and gentling her annoyance.

"You hurt?" he asked her without looking away from the man who'd taken the lead.

She grunted, a noise she hoped he'd interpret as "no". He must have been satisfied because he started into the woods. She stayed at his side, glaring at the wolves as they opened a hole to let her and Nick pass. She glanced back and watched them close the circle again, narrowing around their alpha.

That complex mixture of disgust and fear followed her away from the group.

CHAPTER TEN

They paused a few hundred yards from Nick's truck so Tiana could shift back to her human form before they stepped out into the open spaces around the side road. The instant she was done, Nick wrapped her up in a tight, one-armed hug, desperate to make sure she was okay.

"You're sure you're not hurt?" he asked against her hair as he breathed in her scent.

"I'm fine. Just annoyed." She wrapped her arms around his waist, hugging him back tightly. "I'm so sorry I got you into this."

"My fault. Should have told you about the wolves." He was disgusted with himself for putting her into this terrible position.

She eased back and touched his injured arm. "Broken?"

"It'll heal soon."

"We need to set it so it'll heal right."

"Doctor in town can do that."

He didn't really want to take that option. The doc would notice how fast he healed and might start asking questions. The people of Eirene were generally discreet and left you to your secrets, but something like healing from a broken arm within hours was bound to get the wrong type of attention.

A problem he'd worry about later. Now, he was more concerned with getting Tiana out of the cold.

She refused to move for a moment longer, as she inspected his arm. "I'll set the bone for you," she said, "so the doctor doesn't notice. Every single one of my six brothers has required a bone set at some stage. Most of them more than once. I'm used to it."

His heart beat a little faster with emotions he didn't want to analyze.

"What happened with the two wolves holding you?" He'd seen them both on the ground after he'd knocked the alpha out.

In the middle of his fight, he'd seen one wolf grab Tiana's breast. A rage unlike anything he'd ever experienced had taken hold, and he'd felt the madness lurking in him. He barely remembered the moments that followed as he tore at the alpha. He'd moved too slowly once, after tossing off Corwin's reinforcements, and that had landed him with the broken arm, but he'd barely noticed the break against the darkness swamping him. Her scream had only fired that rage.

A part of him had recognized when she'd shifted and come to guard his back, but most of his logic was lost to the need to destroy those who would threaten her. The only reason he hadn't actually killed Corwin was because his tiger had been aware Tiana wasn't in immediate danger. It was only that instinct that prevented him from breaking the stupid wolf's neck.

She scowled while she continued her inspection, moving from his arm to some of the remaining cuts on his chest. "I was trying to get away to come help you, since some of the other wolves were about to get involved in the fight. It already wasn't fair."

He grunted when she brushed too close to one deep cut, and she grimaced.

"Sorry. Anyway, my guard thought groping me would be a good way to stop me. His mistake."

"What did you do?"

"Let's just say one wolf probably won't be able to have kids and the other's gonna need a knee brace for the next week."

The fear riding him eased under the weight of a pride he had no right to feel. "I didn't know you could fight."

"Alexis has been training a lot of us."

That statement raised many more questions than it answered. "My Alexis? Alexis Tarasova? Former Tracker? Married to Victor Romanov? Three irritating and adorable children?"

She chuckled. "That's the one."

"Who's us? And why is Alexis training you to fight?" Alexis was like a sister to Nick and his brothers. She'd been the Tracker sent to bring his father in for judgment after he'd killed the human. Alexis had taken the Chernikov boys under her wing and been an integral part of their lives ever since. Nick thought he knew everything there was to know about Alexis. Obviously, he was wrong.

"The other tigresses. You remember that thing with Sujin Lee-Bennett years ago?"

How could he forget? The entire community had been rocked by the brutal murder of one of their own—by a human. Ten years later, most tigers were still affected by that loss. "What about it?"

"Well afterward, Elizaveta thought the females should know how to defend themselves better—not just by tiger instinct but with actual training that would work against humans as well as other tigers. So Alexis has been giving self-defense classes ever since."

"For more than ten years? How the hell did I not know this?"

"We haven't been advertising it to the males. You guys don't need to know."

Her chin lifted a little and he had to fight off a smile. How the hell he could smile now, he wasn't sure, but damned if he wasn't impressed with her.

Fuck. He was in so much trouble.

"Come on." He tugged at her. "We need to get back to the truck so you can get some clothes on."

He was exerting a great deal of willpower in keeping his attention above her neck. He wasn't sure he'd be able to keep his needs or instincts in check if he gave himself the chance to study her in all her curvy, naked glory. The glimpses he'd already gotten were enough to dominate his fantasies for the rest of his life.

"I'm fine," she said. "But I do want to get somewhere to set this bone."

Despite his intentions, his emotions and instincts pushed him to a single break in his self-control. He lifted her face with a finger under her chin so she had to look him in the eyes. "You're sure you're not hurt?"

"I'm fine."

She spoke with such annoyance, his willpower dipped a bit lower, swept under by his relief and admiration. He kissed her, a soft touching of the lips, a gentle brush of contact just to assure himself she was okay. The contact sizzled through him, and his tiger rumbled in approval. With effort, he ended the kiss. But the feel of her lips against his followed him back to his truck.

When they reached the vehicle, Tiana helped him get a shirt on over his injured arm, then she slipped into his spare jeans and t-shirt—both of which hung interestingly on her lush figure, in ways that urged him to strip the clothing back off again. She took his keys and motioned him into the front seat.

"I wouldn't put money on Corwin's chances of surviving as alpha," Tiana murmured as she fastened her seatbelt and started the engine.

"Pack business. I don't give a fuck so long as they leave us alone."

"They're still your neighbors. Knowing how this pans out might not be a bad idea."

"I'll worry about it later. I'm sick of wolves right now."

"Yeah. Me, too." She glanced at him briefly. "Let's go

to my motel room to take care of that bone. Better the others in town don't see you like this."

He rested his head against the back of his seat. "Thanks. I know the doc would be discreet, but this will be better."

She was quiet for a few minutes as they bumped over the dirt road. Then she said, "This is that thing you did for the town, isn't it? You dealt with the werewolves for them?"

He sighed.

"What happened, Nick?"

"No big deal. The alpha's crap with money. He got the pack into trouble and thought to fix that trouble by shaking down the town. I settled it."

"How? Not by fighting him."

"I paid him off. We set up the territories—with the town firmly in mine—and agreed if I went into theirs, I'd be subject to a full challenge."

"You didn't go into their territory, though. That was my fault."

"Doesn't matter. The alpha gave me responsibility for any tigers who happened into the pack's lands. I should have told you from the start."

"Why didn't you?"

"Stupid. Didn't want to talk about it."

Which was a half-truth. The town made a big deal of what he'd done, and it always annoyed him. He just had the money to make a problem go away so he could live in peace. He hated the way the townspeople held him up like some fucking hero. So he didn't like to talk about the situation. But the full truth was that he'd been too wound up and distracted by Tiana's presence to consider the risk.

"Stupid," he muttered again. "Should have warned you. My fault you were in that mess." He rolled his head to look at her. "They didn't do anything to you last night?"

"No. I would have done more damage if they'd actually tried to hurt me. The alpha wanted you."

"They didn't give you any clothes."

She snorted. "That stupid bitch who tried to challenge me thought it was funny to keep me naked." She shrugged. "Dumb. They should know I couldn't care less. Must be a prudish pack to even notice."

"You weren't cold?"

"We weren't outside for long. They have a cabin not that far from where they met you. And that wolf who spoke up at the end, he gave me boots, which were nice to keep the chill out since my guards didn't let me move around much once we got to the clearing. I was warm enough for the night, though."

"When did they find you?"

She rolled her eyes. "I went for a run after our date. Obviously, went too far. They picked me up around one a.m."

"I'm so sorry."

"Stop apologizing. It's done."

"Still feel like shit."

"So do I."

"Why? What's wrong?"

She glared at him before focusing on the road again. "I

got you into a fight. The exact thing you're in this town to avoid. I hate that that happened."

"That wasn't your fault."

"Not the point."

She swallowed visibly, and for a horrible moment Nick thought he saw tears in her eyes. He sat up and leaned toward her, but she shook him off.

"Don't. You need to keep that arm still."

He settled back, but something in her tone worried him. He couldn't read her expression or guess what was wrong. There were no hints in her scent. But his muscles tightened with a low level of anxiety that stayed with him all the way to the motel.

CHAPTER ELEVEN

Tiana forced down the anger and tears threatening to spill out. Now that they were out of immediate danger, the full impact of what had happened engulfed her. She'd gotten Nick hurt and forced him into a situation where he had to fight despite what he wanted.

She felt awful. Not so much for this particular fight. This situation had been an accident, a miscommunication. The problem was she had come here purposefully trying to force him back to the Mate Run where he would have to fight again.

Despite the rules of the Run that forbade male challenge fights, she couldn't ignore the reality that if she was here breaking those rules, it was likely the males would break them too and come after Nick—just as he'd warned her they would.

She was in love with him. How could she ask him to go back to that?

He was a magnificent fighter. He'd taken on an angry, vengeful werewolf while he was still in human form and he'd won, coming away with only a broken arm. She knew he'd be able to handle any tiger who challenged him.

But he shouldn't have to. Not when he'd gone out of his way to avoid it all these years. He wanted peace and quiet. He didn't want to fight anymore. What she was asking of him was selfish.

And yet...

If she let him go, if she told him not to run, where did that leave her?

She couldn't face another cycle with tigers she felt nothing for. Not now. The trip to Russia, any other Runs... All of that effort would be pointless because she couldn't bear the idea of being with anyone but Nick.

What was she going to do?

She pulled into the motel lot and parked in the spot in front of her room door, staring at the white walls and dark wood railings of the walkways on the two upper floors. Snow decorated the pitched roof and gave the motel a lovely quaint look. First thing first, she had to make sure his broken bone was lined up and stayed in place while he healed.

She studied the upper story walkways and sidewalk in front of the first floor rooms, the stairs leading between floors, looking for any humans who might see Nick with his broken arm. A small family filed into a room on the third floor, and a solitary man came out of a second floor room. Once the family was inside and the man had driven off, they were clear to go in without any witnesses.

She came around to Nick's side of the truck to help him out, but he was already standing beside the door, steady and sure.

Her heart beat faster at the sight of him, so solid and strong. He was magnificent, wearing jeans and an open flannel shirt, his hair mussed from the fight, his green eyes still bright with residual anger and aggression. A shiver of desire traveled down her spine.

"We need to get inside before anyone else comes out and notices us," she said.

Inside the room, she nodded for him to sit on her bed, then she went to the closet for a scarf. She held it up when she joined him. "For keeping your arm immobilized until the wound heals."

His bone would reknit and be good as new in a few hours. Until then, he'd have to keep it still or risk the bone healing badly.

As she studied the injury with gentle fingers, she asked, "Who's looking after the diner?"

"Jane and one of my other cooks."

"What did you tell them?"

"Jane made me go look for you. I didn't know about the wolves till I got back to my truck and saw their note. I just knew you were missing."

She nodded. "So they don't know…about the wolves?"

"They think the pack is a motorcycle gang, thugs."

"What will we tell them?" She braced herself against the pain she was about to inflict, then took his arm in a firm hold and ensured the bone was in line. He barely flinched. She wasn't sure if that made her feel better or worse. How often had he had to have a bone set? How many injuries had he endured over the years?

"I'll tell them you got lost hiking in the backwoods."

She snorted. "Yeah, right."

"They don't know enough about you to know better."

"Okay. I'll sacrifice my pride this time." She wrapped her scarf around his arm, then stretched it across his chest to keep his arm in place against his side. After tying the scarf off as best she could, she studied her work. "That should do. Just try not to move much for a bit. Are you hungry? You must be after that fight."

"Don't worry about me."

"What do you want to eat?"

"I said…"

"Nick Chernikov, stop arguing with me. I am going to feed you and look after you until your arm heals. Period. Now, what do you want to eat?"

His lips twitched. "Hamburgers will do."

"I'll be right back."

Without bothering to change into her own clothes—because she loved wearing things that smelled so strongly of Nick—she left for the closest fast food restaurant.

The distance from him didn't give her any more clarity. She was still torn between her conscience and her heart. She wanted him and the future they could have together more than she had ever wanted anything in her life. She wanted to have a family with him and make a life here in this town he loved so much.

But she didn't want to force him into fights with the other males.

Maybe she could go to Elizaveta. The elder wasn't allowed to intercede for her grandsons, but if the others broke Mate Run rules by going after Nick, the elder could step in. That was tiger law.

Except if she went to Elizaveta, the elder might realize Tiana had broken Run laws by going to Nick in between cycles. They weren't supposed to be together. If anyone found out she was here with him, he'd be officially banned from the Run for years, maybe forever. She couldn't risk that. Even if he didn't come back for her, he might still want to return one day.

The thought of him running for another tigress made her snarl and her chest ache. Stupid. Irrational. But the pain was real.

By the time she got back with the burgers, she still had no idea what to do. If she continued asking him to return to the Run for her, she'd be asking him to fight. If she left and let him go, she'd lose her one chance at love and a family. She'd still be under pressure by her people to mate, too. She wouldn't be able to stop running.

When she walked back into the room, Nick was leaning against the wooden headboard, flicking through the TV channels so fast she was sure he couldn't possibly tell what was on.

She held up the bags of food. "I hope this is enough. I know it's not as good as the food at the diner."

He snorted. "Nothing around here is."

She'd tasted his food so she had a hard time begrudging

him his pride. She unwrapped the five bacon cheeseburgers she'd bought him and lined them up on paper napkins next to him on the bed by his good hand. Then she settled at the desk with her three hamburgers. The wolves hadn't seen fit to feed her. She could easily have eaten more, but this would take the edge off.

He finished the first burger in three bites and was halfway through the second when he said, "My brothers and I lived off takeout and TV dinners for years after my mom died. My Uncle Erik—the uncle who raised us—was a horrible cook. He tried a few times, then gave up and fed us as best he could from restaurants. I still have trouble eating cereal since that's the only thing we had for breakfast for years."

"Years?"

"It was the only thing Uncle Erik knew how to make. Without burning it."

"Not even frozen waffles or toast?"

"Burned. Burned. He never paid much attention to the food he ate, so figuring out how to feed three growing boys was beyond him."

"But wasn't Mikhail just a baby when..." Since this was the first time he'd brought up his family in casual conversation, she didn't want to break the spell by mentioning his father's crimes aloud. This glimpse into his childhood was fascinating.

"Uncle Erik could handle milk and store bought baby food. Already prepared stuff was right up his alley. Anything that required heat was beyond him. He couldn't even manage the microwave without turning whatever he was trying to cook into a brick." Nick laughed. "By the time I was twelve, I was so sick of the way we ate, I taught myself how to cook. Got a little help from Alexis. Then I learned the rest by trial and error."

"You obviously did a good job." She smiled at his soft expression, the half-smile of good memories.

For some reason, the fact that he had good memories of his childhood came as a relief. He'd been so careful to avoid the topic of family, she'd worried there wasn't much about his childhood he could look back on with any pleasure.

She'd had such a wonderful childhood, such a close relationship with her family, she just couldn't imagine having that all ripped away from her as young as Nick had lost his parents. More than anything, she wanted to give him the kind of happy, loving family life she'd experienced.

"Never thought I'd end up owning a restaurant," he said. "I started cooking out of necessity. Funny how that happens? The perfect thing for you just sort of falls into your lap."

He met her gaze as he spoke and Tiana's heart skipped a beat. She was afraid to read anything into his comment, but oh how she wanted to imagine he was talking about her.

"Six brothers, huh?" he asked.

Tiana shook herself out of the moment of longing and smiled. "All of them very rough and tumble."

"You know they'd kick my ass if they caught us together like this?"

"I'm not planning on telling them. Besides, I just saw you fight. I don't want you and my brothers going at it."

"They'd have every right to kick my ass."

She tried to glare. "My being here isn't any of their business."

He raised his brows but didn't comment. "Older, younger?"

"I'm the third, so two older, four younger."

"Big family."

"My parents were a good match. They fell in love during the Run and are still together all these years later. They're ridiculously cute and mushy."

"Mushy?"

She laughed. "It's kind of disgusting how in love they still are. My mom said she knew the minute she caught his scent, he was the only one for her." Tiana had always wanted that kind of love, but she hadn't actually believed her mom when she said she'd known so quickly. In fact, she'd doubted her mother's story right up to the day she met Nick. She understood her mother a lot better now.

"Most relationships don't work out that way," he said quietly.

"I know. I don't have a lot of illusions, Nick, despite what you might think. Three of my brothers are old enough to take part in Mate Runs. None of them have found a mate. Only one even came close and that tigress ended up choosing a different male on her next Run. I know the kind of relationship my folks have is rare." She held his gaze, steady and sure when she said, "But it does happen. And when it does, it's wonderful."

She'd always believed in the depths of her soul that the kind of love her parents shared was worth fighting for, worth doing whatever it took to have. Now, her fear for Nick complicated her beliefs. She still thought love was worth fighting for, but what if one of the lovers didn't want to fight?

She turned away to finish her food, afraid to show him her confusion.

"Tiana," he murmured. "What's wrong? The wolves…"

"Nothing to do with them." She waved that away. "Though, I will be staying out of their territory now." She winced.

"Then what is it?"

How could she tell him when she didn't know herself? She wasn't sure how to put the complex mix of confused emotions into words he might understand. And even if he did understand, he might use her confusion as an excuse to send her away. She wasn't prepared to give him up yet. She just wasn't sure her conscience would let her keep trying to talk him back into a world he'd abandoned.

Because she had to say something or he'd just keep at her, she admitted, "I'm just tired. I didn't sleep last night."

His brows snapped down in a scowl. "Why the hell didn't you say anything? Come lay down. You need to sleep."

"I can wait until your arm heals. I don't want to crowd you."

"Get into this bed and sleep, Tiana. Now."

The thought of sleeping next to him, of being in a bed so close to him, was a temptation too enticing to resist.

Though she wasn't sure she'd be able to sleep with him so near. Especially while she was still wearing clothes that enveloped her in his scent.

She crawled onto the bed beside him as he tossed the remaining paper napkins onto the nightstand, clearing room for her. She settled on her side, facing him, a pillow bunched up under her head.

"You're sure this isn't going to crowd you? You still have a few hours of healing left."

"Sleep," he ordered.

"Won't Jane be expecting you?"

"I called her already. My backup cook is going to take the dinner shift, too. I don't have anywhere to go or anything to do for the rest of the day. Now rest. And don't argue with me anymore or you're going to piss me off."

She grinned a little and closed her eyes. "Wouldn't want to do that," she mumbled and was rewarded by his low chuckle. That wonderfully relaxed sound, along with the delicious and settling scent of him, went with her into her dreams.

CHAPTER TWELVE

Nick watched her sleep, his chest heavy and tight. He hadn't talked about his childhood with anyone in a long time. Especially not a tigress. Most of his people looked at him and his childhood and saw the bad stuff—his mother's suicide, the status of Nick and his brothers, the crimes his father had committed...

Despite all that, and regardless of the fighting and trouble, he and his brothers had had some good times. They'd spent weeks with Alexis at her cabin in the heart of her territory, a place they were all safe and could just be. More than once they'd had to face their uncle after destroying his kitchen in a food fight. There were quiet runs in the woods. Camping and hunting trips. The chaos of babysitting for Alexis and Victor. The trips to Europe and Russia to experiment with new cooking techniques.

His life was good now, and he'd had good moments over the years, things he could think back on and smile.

But when most tigers looked at him, all they saw was his father.

Too often, that was all Nick saw when he looked in the mirror as well.

He reached out and brushed a lock of hair off Tiana's forehead, trailing a light caress down her cheek. He understood his father much better now. The rage and sorrow… If the wolves had hurt Tiana, Nick knew with certainty that those things would have risen to consume him. He would have torn the entire pack to pieces without thought.

Knowing what he was capable of had always terrified him. Knowing he could tip over into his father's insanity had haunted him his entire life.

He'd touched that place in his fight with Corwin.

He had a choice to make: to continue hiding from that part of himself—which would mean giving up Tiana—or to embrace it, face it fully and accept it.

She was worth it, he realized. She was worth facing his dark heart.

Tatiana Loban-Gupta was the most amazing woman he'd ever met, surprising him and fascinating him in equal measure. He kept imagining taking her to Europe and watching her expression as they ate their way across the continent. Or fantasizing about what she'd look like after sex, with her blonde hair mussed, her dark eyes sleepy and sexy.

But could he ask her to marry him, a man who danced so close to that edge of insanity? She wanted children. What if something happened to her and he fell into that black place, abandoning his children the way his father had? What if he passed his father's weakness down to his own sons? Or his mother's instability to a daughter?

He couldn't escape the truth. He couldn't be a good mate to Tiana, no matter what he wanted. The risk to her was too great.

His tiger didn't want to listen to reason. His tiger looked at her with possessive intent. His mate.

She wasn't anything like his mother, he reminded himself. Hell, she'd learned self-defense and fighting techniques from Alexis. His mother would never have bothered learning how to fight beyond her own instincts.

Tiana was strong. She didn't suffer with depression. She would never take her own life.

Not under normal circumstances. But his mother had been hit with *post-partum* depression on top of her normal depression. Any woman could get that after having a baby. What if that happened to Tiana? What if he didn't see the signs?

He swallowed hard. He'd put the idea of children and a wife out of his head years ago. He couldn't believe he was contemplating opening himself up to that pain again.

Tiana made a soft sound in her sleep and edged a little closer to him, her lips lifting in a smile when she breathed deeply.

As he watched her, what really surprised him was that he was still thinking of giving her up. What kind of idiot was he that he would let this woman go? She was magnificent in so many ways. Fighting for her wouldn't be a challenge. It would be a privilege.

But that didn't solve the darker issue—what if something went wrong and his mind snapped? Could he hope to escape his father's curse? Was he stronger than his father? Did he dare take that chance?

When Tiana woke, Nick was still beside her, his scent wrapping around her like a blanket. Sometime in her sleep, she'd reached out to him, or maybe he'd reached for her, because they were holding hands now. Casually. Easily. As if they always did this in bed.

The rightness of it filled her heart with an ache of longing. She couldn't imagine having this with anyone else. She looked up at Nick. He was watching her. She didn't have any words, not for long moments. He squeezed her hand and she squeezed back.

Finally, she broke the silence. "How's your arm?"

"All healed now."

"Wow, I was asleep for a while. What time is it?"

"After midnight."

"Midnight?" She sat up, without releasing his hand. "Why didn't you wake me?"

"You needed the rest. I didn't have anywhere to go."

"But you must be starving! Give me a minute to use the bathroom and I'll go out and get some more food."

He scowled. "I'm healed now. I can feed myself."

"But…"

"Besides, there's nothing open at this hour. Not anywhere nearby, anyway."

She frowned. "But you need food."

His scowl softened and a contemplative look replaced it. He was still holding her hand, more tightly now, as if she might pull away. "How about we go to the diner? I can make us a late dinner."

"No. You're not cooking for me—not after you had to fight for me this afternoon."

"I like cooking. It's relaxing. And I'd like to cook for you."

"It's too late to open the diner."

"It's my place. I can do what I want."

"But…" She shook her head, but he cupped her cheek with his free hand and stilled the motion.

Her breath caught. The feel of his hand on her face was a kind of torture. Because she wanted to lean forward and kiss him so badly her entire body vibrated with the need. So close. So easy. Hell, they were already in bed. Her stupid "no sex" rule could take a hike after what they'd gone through today.

Yet… Yet. Her conscience still poked at her.

She told the bitch to shut up, leaned in, and kissed Nick. He met her halfway, his kiss hungry, hard, and so, so right. She wrapped herself around him, half in his lap before she knew what she was doing.

He didn't argue with her or point out all the reasons this was a bad idea. He didn't pull away. And she couldn't resist him. His scent rose up to meld with hers, creating that unique combination that was more delicious than any food could be. Catnip, she thought. She dragged her mouth from his to kiss her way down the column of his throat, savoring the salty male taste. His groan made her smile as she dipped lower, nudging aside his still open flannel shirt so she could get at his chest.

He tangled his fingers in her hair, holding her tightly as she explored with her lips. She couldn't taste him enough, every lick, every kiss only fueling her hunger. She pushed his shirt over his shoulders so she could explore his muscles.

When he sat up to remove the shirt, she leaned back and dragged her own shirt over her head. Her breasts felt heavy, her nipples tight in the cool air. His gaze dropped to her chest, and he reached for her before she'd finished pulling the shirt off.

He cupped her breast, weighing it in his palm, and she moaned. Without conscious thought, she took her other nipple between her fingers, squeezing and pinching. The sound he made was nothing she'd heard from a man before, all deep, husky and desperate, and his grip tightened as he watched her.

Then he dipped and took the nipple she was playing with into his mouth. She moaned, her body lighting up with need. His mouth on her was electric, sending shocks of sensation to her core. He sucked hard, giving little nips in between until she was gasping and begging for more.

Pushing her back onto the mattress, he turned his attention to her other breast. She writhed beneath him, her whole body pulsing and hot. She held his head in place with one hand and unbuttoned her jeans with the other, pushing and wiggling to remove the last of her clothes. She didn't want anything between them. He never took his mouth from her as he shucked off his own jeans.

She wanted to take time to savor him, naked and beautiful, but she was lost to the feel of him, and she didn't want him to stop what he was doing.

When he moved from her breast to her stomach, she trembled with so much desire she didn't think her body could contain it.

"You're so fucking beautiful," he growled against her skin as he kissed his way over her rounded tummy. "So lush and sexy. And delicious."

He breathed deeply, licked a circle around her navel, then nibbled the skin on her hipbone, a gesture that made her buck. She felt lush and sexy and beautiful with Nick. Her body was heavy and pulsed in time with her rapid heartbeat. When Nick licked a line down her inner thigh, she wanted to scream. She gripped her own breasts again, pulling at her nipples in hard tugs, trying to ease some of the tension building in her core. Nothing helped. She was wet and desperate, and completely at his mercy.

He kissed her inner thigh, then bit down hard. She did cry out this time and pinched her nipples harder.

"Yes," he said. "I love watching your hands on your breasts. Don't stop."

She couldn't find her voice to answer him. He pushed her thighs farther apart, then settled his mouth against her wet heat, licking her once gently. Then he spread her with his fingers and licked into her, and Tiana lost her mind. She panted and tried to hold back her orgasm, to savor the feel of his tongue on her, but he didn't make it easy. He licked hard, pushing her, driving her toward a total loss of control.

"Nick…" His name came out as a harsh moan. The scent of her own desire mixed with their tangled essences, and it pushed her over the sharp, hot edge. She arched up, every muscle tight, and then her body exploded into a rippling spasm of release so intense she stopped breathing for an instant. When she dropped back down, she was limp and shivering, hot and satisfied, but still needy.

"More," she growled. "More of you." She pushed him onto his back and took his hard cock into her mouth before he'd settled. His answering hiss fueled her, fed her. She pulled away just long enough to whisper, "You taste so good."

He shivered as her breath hit the tip of his cock. "Tiana, you're going to kill me."

She smiled, then she took him in her mouth again. She wanted to make him come too, to take him this way. But she wasn't sure she'd survive the time it took for him to get hard again before she took him inside. His muscles were tight under her, so solid and hard. He panted, and the harder she sucked the harsher he breathed. One hand tightened in her hair, the other ripped at the blanket beside him. She pushed him as far as she dared, reluctant to lose the taste of him, but unable to resist having all his pulsing thickness inside her.

He didn't complain when she took her mouth from him, just watched her with dark, hooded eyes, his jaw tight. She straddled him, positioned his cock at her entrance, and dropped down in a single fast move. He was thick and perfect, filling her in a way she'd never experienced. For several moments, she rocked gently, just savoring him.

He gripped her hips, his fingers digging into her skin, and he growled again, his voice harsh and deep. "Move if you don't want me to take over."

She laughed and did as he ordered, rising up and dropping down with a groan. His cock stretched her and the friction started another orgasm building, this one deeper and richer. She fucked him as hard and fast as she'd wanted to since first catching his scent. Her breasts bounced with her movement, the sensation adding to her growing tension. She watched him as he watched her. The heat in his eyes, the emotion and barely held control, drove her faster, harder.

This time she held her own orgasm at bay, focusing on his pleasure, waiting to see him break. When he did, he roared her name and Tiana let go, her inner muscles clenching before everything tightened and burst apart.

As the ebbs of her orgasm eased, she folded over him, still gently pumping her hips as she came back down.

"Oh, my," she murmured into his neck, then licked his skin because tasting him felt so natural and necessary. "That...worked."

His chuckle was harsh and breathless. He tightened his arms around her waist and hugged her, shivering when she licked him again.

"Fuck," he breathed.

She sat up enough to look at him. "What?"

"I want you again already. And you're not even in estrous."

He sounded so awed and appalled in equal measure, she laughed. "Told you we had good chemistry."

His groaned laugh was a little pained. "Combustible chemistry."

"I'm not near done with you yet," she said. "But I might need a few more minutes before we start again."

"God." He held her tight and rolled her onto her back. "You're going to kill me, and I'll die with a stupid grin on my face."

"We'll go together."

He kissed her, deep and gentle, but still with the heat lurking just at the edge. She gave herself to the kiss, forcing back any thoughts. She was too happy, too content to think or consider their future. She'd worry about it tomorrow. Or maybe the next day. For now, Nick was hers and she wanted to wallow in the dream that this was their forever.

When he pulled back suddenly and rolled out of bed, she gasped. "What's wrong?"

"Nothing. I want to feed you. Come on." He tugged her to her feet and took her to the bathroom so they could clean up.

His attention had her body humming again in moments, but he didn't give in to her wordless pleas. Instead, he found clothes for her in the closet and actually dressed her —just a shirt and jeans; no underwear or bra. She felt so sexy under his ministrations she wasn't about to argue. And the lack of underwear would make it easier to strip and fuck him again at the soonest possible moment.

"Where are we going?" she asked as he held his truck door for her. "The diner?"

"My house. I want to cook for you in my home."

Her heart jumped and her throat tightened. She was lost. His. Completely and entirely. He was going to break her heart. But in that moment, she decided the pain was worth it. Nick was worth it.

CHAPTER THIRTEEN

Nick let Tiana into his house and had to fight a possessive growl of satisfaction at having her there. *His.* He couldn't deny it anymore. He was completely lost to her. Having her in his home, filling it with her scent, only reinforced that sense of possessiveness. And resignation.

"What would you like to eat?" he asked as he took her coat and hung it on one of the hooks by his door.

"Whatever you have is fine. Just no eggs." She wrinkled her nose.

"I remember." He grinned, feeling like a love-struck fool, but not really caring. "I've got steaks?"

"Meat! Perfect."

"Make yourself comfortable." He motioned to his living room. "You want something to drink?"

"Water would be nice. Thanks."

As she wandered into his living room, he took to the comfort of his kitchen. Cooking for her felt…intimate in a way cooking had never felt before. Some soul-deep instinct drove him to feed and care for her, make sure she was comfortable and content.

Thoughts of his father haunted him as he pulled the meal together. He remembered his dad doing similar things for his mother—cooking for her, making sure she was comfortable, looking after her and spoiling her. To this day, Nick still wasn't sure how his father had missed his mother's depression when he seemed—to a nine-year-old boy anyway—so devoted and attentive.

Tiana is nothing like your mother, he reminded himself.

But he was oh so much like his father.

He was about to call her in to eat when he felt her come up behind him. She wrapped her arms around his waist and leaned around him to look at the simple grilled steaks he had resting.

"Those look and smell delicious."

"You smell delicious."

She kissed his shoulder, her chuckle vibrating against his skin. The sensation traveled straight to his cock, but he wanted her fed first.

They took their plates to his dining room table, a place he usually reserved for paying bills, and chatted about easy things: movies, cooking, her work, and the townspeople. She smiled a lot. He laughed more than he had in years. The comfort, the rightness of it, wasn't lost on him.

The ephemeral nature of that peace wasn't lost on him, either.

Had his parents experienced this in the beginning? Was this where the madness started?

And could he escape the consequences now, or was it too late?

As soon as she finished eating, his self-control buckled. "Dishes can wait," he said as he pulled her to her feet and into his arms. She fell into his kiss without resistance. He loved that about her.

They stumbled up the stairs, petting and kissing as they went. More than once, Nick thought they might not make it to the bedroom. At the top of the stairs, he pushed her against the nearest wall so he could feel her entire body pressed against his. He pulled her top off and tossed it behind him, his gaze dropping to the delicious fullness of her breasts.

"I love your body," he muttered, before taking her nipple into his mouth.

She lifted up on her toes and clenched at his shoulders, panting as he sucked hard. She was so sensitive, so responsive, he wondered if he could make her come like this. Tempting. But maybe later. There was so much he wanted to do with her, to her, and he had a bed just a few feet away. With a final lick, he released her nipple and grabbed her hand, tugging her to his room, and his bed.

Desperation like he'd never experienced pushed him. He actually ripped her jeans dragging them off, but he couldn't find it in him to care. He needed her naked, needed to feel and explore her glorious body. He needed to bathe in her scent and fill himself with her.

Years of want and denial had left him so vulnerable to

her. He'd imagined having her in his bed, just like this, so often it was like living in a dream. Except her moans were real. Her scent was real. And those desperate little sounds she made when he kissed her inner thigh, when he licked into her, were so much better than anything he could have imagined.

"Nick!" Her voice was deep and husky, the sound fueling his lust.

He couldn't taste her enough. No spice, no dish, no food had ever tasted so perfect. When she tightened and trembled, he gripped her closer and pushed her to an orgasm that had her shaking against him.

"I could spend years just like this," he said against her thigh. Sweat dripped between her breasts, drawing his attention. He moved up her body, kissing her as he went, savoring her little jumps and gasps when he hit sensitive spots. "I want to know everything, find everything that makes you come."

"You've made one hell of a start," she moaned as he took her nipple into his mouth again.

"Not enough. This is going to take some time."

She chuckled, but the sound was strained and tight. "Fine. Just... Oh!"

He smiled against her skin. Apparently, her waist was as sensitive as her breasts. He filed that away for future use, then rose up to kiss her. She wiggled under him, pushing and tugging to get him where she wanted him. Then she wrapped her legs around his hips and arched up to bump against his cock. Her invitation was clear, and he wanted to be inside her so much, it never crossed his mind to resist.

She was hot and wet, her body stretching and taking him as if they made love all the time. He lifted onto his arms enough to watch her as he rocked against her, into her. The way her eyes fluttered open and closed, the way her lips parted, the way she gasped and panted, the feel of her fingers digging into his arms, everything about her was perfect, beautiful…*his*.

Her orgasm tightened her inner muscles around him and dragged him toward his own release too quickly. He held out just long enough to watch her come, the flush that rose across her chest and into her cheeks, the way her jaw clenched, the sound of her cry reverberating through his bedroom. Then he let go and followed her, unable to resist her or refuse her anything now.

After, he held her close, pulling his blankets up around them and tucking her head under his chin so he could savor her scent. He didn't want this moment to end. He certainly didn't want to think about the future.

She rolled a little to look out the window, then groaned. "Almost sunrise. You have to work today?"

"I'll be fine."

"I should have let you sleep earlier."

"Right. That's what I wanted. Sleep."

She snorted. "You need to sleep now. At least a few hours."

He didn't really want to sleep. He was afraid he'd wake up and find this had all been a vivid hallucination. "Okay," he said. "I'll sleep. But I want to wake up with you here."

She snuggled against him. "Not going anywhere."

He tightened his hold, to keep her close and to reassure

himself that she was really there. Then he closed his eyes and gave over to the exhaustion he'd refused to acknowledge. Their combined scents stayed with him, sending him into the most restful sleep he'd ever had.

CHAPTER FOURTEEN

Nick didn't want to wake Tiana when he rose for work, so he left her a note by the bed and a light breakfast in the kitchen.

In between cooking, he had to answer questions about Tiana's wellbeing more than once. He realized with no little surprise that the people of Eirene were adopting her, making her one of their own already. She hadn't even been here a week, yet everyone was concerned for her and spoke of her as if she was already a town fixture.

He could keep her here, wake up to her scent on his skin every day, keep her delectable body pressed against his, and savor her sighs and moans and laughs and growls each night. He could claim her as his, marry her, and have a family with her here in this place he felt so at home. The temptation was overwhelming. All he had to do was return to the Mate Run, beat off the other males, and get her pregnant. Then she'd be his. No one could dispute his claim.

Easier said than done.

Also not the real problem.

The specter of his father's madness hung over him throughout the breakfast shift. Fear for the delicate, easily shattered future he wanted with Tiana dogged him through lunch.

He went home after the lunch hour to find her, trying not to think about all the problems they faced. He was surprised she hadn't come into the diner for lunch, so an edge of worry followed him home, taking precedence over his other fears. He didn't think the wolves would actually come into his territory to get her, and he couldn't smell them anywhere nearby. He could feel her still in his home so he knew she hadn't gone off anywhere. But after yesterday, he was edgy and anxious to be with her again.

"Tiana?" he called as soon as he stepped inside. He opened himself to her and realized she was in his small office just off the dining room.

"Back here," she said.

Something in her voice had him hurrying to her, worry making him frown.

He rounded the door and immediately glanced around the small room, looking for any threat. He couldn't scent or feel anything. As far as he could see, she was alone and safe. He faced her, about to ask what was wrong when he noticed a piece of paper in her hands. For several moments, he had no idea what she'd find so interesting in here. Receipts for the diner?

Then he realized—he'd left the box out, the one with all her emails and letters in it.

"You have everything here," she said, her voice husky. "Emails printed out. Everything I sent. You kept it all."

He blew out a breath and put his hands on his hips. What could he say?

"Why? If you weren't going to run, if you weren't going to even write back, why save all this?"

"Fuck. I don't know. They were from you."

"Oh, Nick."

Her bottom lip trembled and panic shot through him. If she cried, she'd break him.

Instead, she set down the letter she'd been holding and hugged him, tightly. He hugged back instinctively, then with a lot more emotion, his hands clenching the material of her shirt.

Again the temptation rose. He could have her, keep her, make her his.

"I love you," she whispered.

Another jolt of emotion roared through him. But before he could form enough presence of mind to actually speak, she pulled back and looked him in the eyes.

"Don't say anything. Not now. Just... You need to know how I feel, but I don't expect..." She shook her head and kissed him.

Need took him instantly, mixing into a volatile brew with his other emotions. He held her so tight, if she'd been human he might have broken her. But Tiana wasn't the type to be easily broken. She was strength and passion and everything he'd never thought to hope for, everything he'd believed he couldn't have.

When she pulled his shirt off, he couldn't object. He was too busy tugging off her clothes.

"Why didn't you come to the diner?" he asked as he pulled her pants down. She was wearing a pair of his sweats and the realization made his head spin.

"You ripped my jeans last night, and I wasn't sure you'd want me to show up at the diner wearing your clothes."

The thought of her strolling into his restaurant wearing his clothing, things covered in his scent, made every possessive cell in his body roar with triumph. Aloud, he said, "I wouldn't have minded."

She smiled and tugged him up so she could push his jeans off. He'd barely toed his boots off and stepped out of his jeans when she gripped his cock. All thought dissolved under the exquisite feel of her hand on him.

He had to be inside her. Now. It was beyond desperate. It was as important as his next breath. Just the few hours he'd been away from her had been too much.

How the hell could he let her go when he couldn't stand to be away from her for half a day?

He lifted her and settled her over his erection. She wrapped her legs around his hips, wiggling closer. Her movements drove him mad. He spun to brace her against the nearest wall, then slid into her. Being inside her heat was like coming home, but a home he'd never experienced before, a place of safety, security, balance, freedom. Love.

Groaning into her neck, he held her for a few moments, just savoring the feel of her. She nipped his shoulder, a none-too-gentle bite, and his blood fired. He stroked into her in a hard, steady rhythm, not fast but not slow. Relentless. He licked the pulse in her throat, and she shivered, a trembling he felt all the way to his cock.

He rocked into her until she panted, until she pleaded, and still he didn't increase his pace. Her entire body clenched, her arms and legs clamping around him, her back arching, pressing her full breasts into his chest. He squeezed her ass and pumped until her tense muscles shook. Then he pulled back to watch her come—a sight he would never grow tired of. She was the most stunning thing he'd ever seen. When she shattered, she gasped his name, her body jumping and shivering against him.

The feel and sight of her orgasm broke his control. He pumped harder, faster until his own release ripped through him, robbing him of everything but a sense of her.

After he settled enough to be aware of his surroundings again, he hugged her, breathing in their combined scents. Emotions beyond his ability to name wrapped around his chest and held tight. He refused to think about it. He was too content, too at peace. He just wanted to savor that for a little bit longer.

He released her enough that she could stand but kept his arms around her as she wobbled.

She smiled, an almost shy expression, when she said, "Shaky legs."

"Is that a good thing?"

"Oh, yeah."

Though he would have preferred to keep her naked, they both slipped back into their clothes. Watching her dress was as sexy as stripping her—especially when she was wearing his clothes.

"You must be starving," he said. "Or did you make yourself something to eat?" He walked her out of his office to the kitchen, keeping his arm around her waist.

"What time is it?" she asked.

"After two."

Her stomach growled in response and she grimaced. "I lost track of time. I am pretty hungry."

"Great. I get to cook for you again."

"That's great?"

He took her face in his hands and kissed her lightly. "I love cooking for you." He dropped his hold and contemplated his closed refrigerator. "What would you like? I have some leftover chicken. I could make a mean sandwich with that."

"Perfect. But…"

"What?"

"You've been cooking all day. I really don't want to put you out."

"Stop, or you'll piss me off. What did I just say?"

She grinned that shy smile again and shrugged. "Fine. But can I help?"

He put her to work washing vegetables while he prepped the chicken, cheese and bread. Working with her in his kitchen, preparing a meal, felt so natural, so…inevitable.

They ate in the dining room again, and he told her about his morning and all the people asking after her. "They were worried."

"That's very sweet of them. I'm surprised they care."

"They're good people."

"Yes. They are."

After the meal, Tiana sat back and patted her tummy with a satisfied smile. Then she yawned. Her eyes widened. "Sorry. You'd think after sleeping most of the morning away, I wouldn't be tired now. Guess the big meal did me in."

"Just the meal?" He raised his brows and she laughed, a sound that charmed him. He could spend hours listening to her laugh and enjoying the way her shoulders and breasts shook with her amusement.

A low level hum of desire wove through his gut. He just couldn't get enough of her. He was about to pull her back up to his bed when her expression changed, her lips flattening.

"What's wrong?" He reached across the table for her hand, but she pulled back. Something close to terror pierced his chest. "Tiana. What is it?"

She swallowed and stood, pacing the length of the small dining room twice before stopping in front of the table again. Uncertain of her mood, he rose to face her, bracing himself for… Well, he wasn't sure, but he felt like he needed to meet whatever she had to say standing.

"Nick…" Hesitance made her brow crease. "I've made things…complicated by being here."

"Wasn't that the point?" He tried to smile to lighten the mood, but she didn't smile back.

"If anyone finds out I'm here, what we've done…"

"No one will."

"I'm going to leave," she blurted.

He opened his mouth to object, but she raised a hand to silence him.

"I'm going to leave. Now. And in a week and a half, I'm going to run."

He held her gaze, waiting. He knew he wouldn't be able to turn her down if she asked him to run again. She was his. He'd be damned if he'd let another tiger have her now. But the specter of his father hung over his shoulder, and fear kept him silent.

"If you come to my Run, I'm yours," she continued. "I love you. There won't ever be anyone else for me."

Hearing the declaration again made his chest swell. He started to nod, but again she stopped him.

"Wait, please, let me finish. If you don't come to the Run, I will understand. I mean it. I won't be angry. I won't begrudge you the decision. It *has* to be your decision. I don't want you to feel pressured anymore. Don't, don't say anything right now. I want you to take some time. You need to really think, really consider what it'll mean to come back to the Run, to return to our world."

"Have you considered it? Have you really thought about what it'll mean, having me back, being my mate?"

She blew out a breath, rocking gently from foot to foot as if standing still was beyond her. "I've thought of nothing else since I first caught your scent. I've made my choice, and I'm happy with it. But I won't force anything on you. I'm...I'm sorry I tried. I didn't think about what I was doing at the time, just that I wanted you and couldn't let you go. I still do."

He wanted her, too. But he had to know, "If I don't run, what will you do?"

"I'll talk to the elders about alternatives."

"Alternatives?" A growl crept into his voice without his permission. If she thought he'd give her up to another tiger now…

"Maybe artificial insemination. I still want children. My brothers can help me raise them." She shrugged. "I'll still be contributing to our population. No one will be able to complain too much."

"You think they'll allow that?"

"It's either that or nothing. This is going to be my last Mate Run. Three years is long enough."

Nick blinked. No one had ever given up on the Run before. Alexis refused to run back in her day, but no tigress had ever tried and then decided she'd had enough without ever once finding a mate. It was unprecedented. Would the elders even allow it?

"I'd better go," Tiana said, pulling him out of his thoughts. "I need to pack."

Another bolt of panic tightened his gut. He desperately wanted to keep her here, to maintain this illusion of peace and happiness they'd built. "You don't have to leave now. Stay until tomorrow."

She smiled, but her mouth wobbled. "If I stay, I might never leave. Then we really will get into trouble."

She kissed him gently on his cheek, and her scent wrapped around him in delicious perfection. Before he could force his brain to function, she grabbed her coat and hurried out the door.

Several minutes passed as he stood in the dining room, stunned by her sudden absence. Then he remembered they'd taken his car last night. Hers was still at the motel. He charged after her, intent on at least driving her back, but as soon as he took the time to sense for her, he realized she was already miles away, running at top shifter speed.

He stood in the cold for a long time, until he couldn't feel her anymore, until even his warm body started to shiver with the chill.

Then he went back inside—to think.

CHAPTER FIFTEEN

Nick was still thinking a week later, sitting in the quiet dark on his small front porch, when one of the wolves joined him—the one who'd spoken for the pack after the alpha had gone down.

Nick considered him without speaking. He'd caught the wolf's scent as soon as he entered Eirene, but Nick didn't smell any others, so he was prepared to give the werewolf some leniency for coming into his territory unannounced.

The man was taller than Corwin, close to Nick's own six foot three inches, and thick with muscle beneath casual jeans and a dark colored ski jacket. His blue eyes were dark and hooded in the dim light from inside Nick's house. His jaw muscles flexed as he stared back at Nick.

Finally, the man dropped his gaze—a wolf sign of submission—and said, "I'm alone."

"I know. Why are you here?"

"Thought you might want to know what happened with

our former alpha and how that affects the situation between you and the pack."

Nick raised his brows at the "former". Everything about the man's scent conveyed non-aggression so Nick gestured to the other seat on the porch. "You want a beer?"

The wolf shook his head. "My name's Adam, by the way. Adam Walsh."

Nick shook his hand—a human greeting he'd made habit over the last five years—then Adam took a seat.

"Is your alpha dead?" A deposed alpha wasn't left alive in a typical werewolf pack. Changes of allegiance required blood. And death was the only way to replace an alpha.

Adam nodded. "My brother's the new alpha."

Nick blinked, then frowned. He'd assumed Adam was in charge now since he was here.

"I'm his beta," Adam said. "He sent me to speak for him and the pack."

"You looking for more money?"

"We didn't know Chris made that arrangement with you. We didn't even know how bad the financials of the pack were. When he started taking some of the more aggressive wolves into Eirene and harassing the townspeople, we thought he was... Well, let's just say it wasn't outside his behavior. Those of us who didn't approve also didn't have any cause to see it as something unusual. It wasn't until your fight that we realized what had happened."

"What excuse did he give for ceding some of your territory to a tiger?"

"He didn't give an excuse. Just said he'd made a sweet

deal with a tiger shifter. But he didn't explain it. Ordered us to avoid certain boundaries from then on."

"And you just bought that?" Nick didn't know that much about the workings of a werewolf pack beyond the basic structure, but he found it hard to believe none of them bothered to dig into the alpha's "sweet deal" with a strange shifter.

Adam shrugged, but his lip lifted in a faint snarl. "Packs aren't typically included in the decisions of their alphas. That's why there's a beta—to mitigate and balance alpha decisions, to be the voice of reason or dissent if necessary. That way the rest of the pack knows what's being done is for the best, with the pack interest in mind. Unfortunately, the ingrained instinct to follow without question can get us into trouble when we have an alpha like Chris."

"How'd he last so long, if some of you had doubts he was best for the pack?"

Adam snorted. "He was the son of our former—beloved —alpha. Doug Corwin requested we give his son our loyalty, so we did."

"Stupid." Nick had some loyalty to his people, even now, and he understood loyalty to family, at least where his brothers were concerned, but blindly following a bad leader in the name of a dead one?

"I'm not here to debate our stupidity," Adam growled.

Nick raised his hands, palms out. He didn't really care either, outside of how this change in leadership would affect his relationship with the pack.

Adam let out a sigh. "Sorry. Sore spot. We kept expecting Chris to be more like his father once he took over. His father was a brilliant alpha. One of the best we've ever had. We *wanted* the son to be like the father. They even looked alike. But lineage doesn't always make the man. At least not in this case."

Nick felt like he'd taken a gut punch. He blinked, staring into the dark night beyond his porch, as the beta's words rolled through him. "Lineage doesn't always make the man."

"Anyway," Adam said, getting back to business, "our new alpha wants to keep the boundaries you set up with Chris. Your territory won't be disputed."

Nick forced himself out of his personal upheaval to ask, "Why?"

"You paid for it," he said simply. "You basically bought the land. It's yours."

Nick hadn't actually thought of it that way before. He'd viewed the payoff as a bribe to get the werewolves to leave the town alone. But if the new leadership wanted to view it as payment for land, he was happy to oblige.

"That said, we're still in a financial fix. Chris had no sense when it came to money. He spent like he was a king and left us in debt. Again."

"And this has to do with me, how?"

"We'd like permission to come into your territory for commercial reasons."

"Commercial reasons?"

"We have a few businesses in Vail, which help support the pack. You get day tourists here. Especially in the winter. We'd like to set up another two businesses here."

"How, if you're in debt?"

"Not your concern. We just need permission to come and go from the town."

"There are other places to establish businesses. Why here?"

"Cheap overheads. Decent traffic. And thanks to word spreading about the food in your diner, more and more tourists are making trips to Eirene. You haven't noticed the increase?"

He had, but it hadn't crossed his mind that it had anything to do with his diner. The people here were smart and industrious. The town was charming and quaint. Why wouldn't people want to visit?

"You planning on opening something to compete with current businesses? I don't want anyone here hurt." Nick was very protective of his adoptive town. He wasn't about to allow Eirene to be overrun by wolves if they were going to put people who lived here out of work.

"Nothing like that. We've started a hydroponic farm. We want to open a place to sell what we grow."

That got Nick's attention. He was always looking for new suppliers for the restaurant. "You said two businesses."

"My sister is…good with clothes." Adam frowned a bit. "She designs stuff. She wants a boutique of her own but can't compete in Vail yet. We thought Eirene would be a good place to start."

Intrigued, Nick spent the next hour discussing options with Adam. They came to an agreement which allowed a limited number of wolves to come into Nick's territory regularly, so long as they agreed to hire local people to work in their shops.

Over the course of the discussions, Nick decided he liked the pack's new beta. He was smart, reasonable, and down to earth. If the alpha was anything like his brother, the pack was in good hands now.

Adam's words came back to Nick then. "Lineage doesn't always make the man." Nick thought about his own brothers. They'd all come from the same heritage, but Dom and Mitch were both strong, loyal, decent men. They'd escaped their father's defects somehow.

Nick was afraid to even consider that maybe he had, too.

But he'd felt the lurking insanity in his fight with Chris Corwin, fighting for Tiana. He wasn't sure he could trust himself *not* to be like his father.

Nick pushed the confused thoughts to the back of his mind and focused on his discussion with Adam. Eventually, they moved from business talk into lighter stuff, and Adam finally took Nick up on that beer. Nick, for his part, embraced the reprieve from his own thoughts. He'd barely gotten through the dinner shift tonight without burning his restaurant down because of inattention. Tiana filled his head, and fear haunted him.

"Where's your woman?" Adam asked, shattering Nick's momentary peace.

"She had to get home."

"You want to talk about it?"

"Nope."

"Fair enough. Will say, she's a brave one. Didn't even balk when our less upstanding wolves tried to bait her." Adam smiled. "She rolled her eyes at them. Thought she might end up in a fight well before we met with you. Not sure she wouldn't have won those fights, too. She's got some skills."

Since she'd been training with Alexis, Nick wasn't surprised.

"I'd better get back." Adam set his empty bottle down on the porch and stood. "Good luck with your woman."

"Thanks." Nick stood, too. "Good luck with getting your pack healthy again."

Adam snorted. "Thanks. I'll be in touch."

Nick waited on the porch until he was sure the werewolf had left town. Then he went inside.

He sat at his desk chair and opened the box of letters and emails from Tiana, the box she'd discovered just before telling him she loved him. He could still hear her sweet, husky voice murmuring those words in his ear.

He was absolutely terrified of ruining that love, of destroying her with his love.

Staring at the box, he was no closer to a decision about running, but he was absolutely certain of one thing. He was in love with Tiana. He belonged to her, heart and soul.

Would that be enough? Would it be too much?

And could he really let her go now, even for her own good?

CHAPTER SIXTEEN

Tiana answered her door on the second knock. She knew it was Ethan, one of her older brothers, but she didn't really want to talk to him. Unfortunately, he didn't take the hint and go away when she ignored his first knock.

"Why are you here?" she asked the moment she opened the door.

"Hi to you, too." Ethan snorted and moved past her without waiting for an invitation.

She scowled after him, then closed the door with a thunk.

All her brothers resembled their father, as was typical for tiger shifters, but Ethan Gupta looked the most like him. He was very handsome with beautiful caramel-colored skin she'd always envied, dark hair and eyes, and the kind of charm they'd all been certain would land him a tiger mate. In fact, of all the brothers, Ethan had been the one everyone thought would end up mated.

She'd often wondered if that pressure had been hard on him, but he'd never discussed it with his little sister.

"What do you want?" she asked, following him into her living room. She had her laptop open on the coffee table where she'd been trying to concentrate on work emails—and failing miserably. He tried to look at the screen and she slammed it shut. "Nosey. Why are you here?" she repeated.

"You have another Run coming up," he said, dropping onto the couch and patting the cushion next to him.

She groaned. "I know. I know."

"We're worried about you. All of us."

"Yeah, well…" She sighed and sat next to him. "I guess I should warn you. This is going to be my last Run."

He frowned. "Why?"

"I've been running for three years."

"There's still options. That trip to Russia…"

She shook her head. "I can't. Not now." She pressed her lips together. Damn, she hadn't meant to say that. Her brother's narrowed eyes confirmed he knew her slip was meaningful.

"What's happened?" He sat up a little higher. "No one's hurt you?"

"No. Nothing like that." She patted his knee and he relaxed, but only a little. "It's just…" She sighed. "Fine. I'm in love."

His eyebrows rose so high, she might have laughed if she wasn't still so heart sore.

"In love?" he said. "With who? A human?"

"No. Fortunately. I'm in love with a tiger."

"But, Tiana, that's great! What's the problem?"

"He's a Chernikov."

Ethan slumped against the couch back. "Shit."

"Exactly."

"Which one? Not Mikhail? He's with someone now."

"Nikolai."

Ethan nodded, but his mouth turned down in a frown.

"You don't like him?"

"No, it's not that. Nikolai doesn't run. None of the Chernikovs have run for years."

"I know."

"How the hell did you even meet Nikolai? How could you possibly be in love with him?"

"Long story, most of which you don't want to know."

He looked like he might argue, then he shook his head. "You're right. I don't. You're in serious trouble, though."

"Yup."

"He's not going to run."

"Actually, he…might." She still wasn't confident Nick would show. She thought he might, despite everything that held him back. She hoped what was between them was enough. But a niggling of doubt still taunted her.

"What have you done?" Ethan shook his head when she opened her mouth. "No. Right. I don't want to know." He blew out a breath. "You know, even if he runs, the others aren't going to just let him be."

"I know," she wailed. "It's not fair. He's allowed to run."

"Since when did fair enter into life?"

The bitterness in his voice made her look, really look at him. His eyes held…sadness. His scent even carried a faint hint of something that spoke of despair. "What's happened to you, Ethan?" she asked, suddenly worried for him.

"We're talking about you right now." Before she could push him, he rushed on. "Listen, taking on a Chernikov, even if he does run, is going to be a tough life. Are you sure? You really love him?"

"I do. And I understand what I'm getting into. But it's possible he won't run and this is all moot. Either way, after this cycle, I'm done with the Run."

"What if the other males try to chase him off?"

She growled, a sound that surprised them both, it was so full of anger. "I will kick the ass of any tiger who tries to run Nick off. He's mine."

"Wow. That's some fierce attitude, little sister."

"Shut up." She scowled at him.

He laughed and some of the sadness that had crept into his eyes lightened. "You're determined to have Nikolai—if he runs?"

"I am. He's the only one I want."

Ethan pursed his lips and considered her, stretching his arm along the back of the couch and tilting his head to one side. "Maybe we can do something to…help matters."

She sat up straighter. "What do you have in mind?"

"Let's call the rest of the clan."

For the first time since leaving Eirene, Tiana felt a shiver of excitement and determination fire in her blood. She grinned at Ethan and snatched up her cellphone.

CHAPTER SEVENTEEN

Tiana knew the instant Nick entered the Mate Run territory and her heart soared. He'd come! She'd hoped and been afraid to hope. She'd wanted and felt selfish for the wanting. But he'd made his choice. He was here.

Giddy excitement made her rock from foot to foot as she opened her senses to all the tigers in the area. There were a lot more males than normally took part in a single Run, but that wasn't unusual for hers. She stood where she was and waited for the males to head toward her, most of her focus on Nick. She couldn't care less about the rest. Every part of her hungered for Nick, turned toward him. Her estrous heightened her senses, lust rode her hard, and all of that emotion and longing was centered on a single male.

He was here for her.

To observe the conventions, she couldn't just stand here

until Nick reached her, despite the fact that she wanted to. She really needed to make him chase her a little. The idea caught the fire already burning through her blood and made her nerves tingle. Oh, she would enjoy having Nick chase her. She was going to enjoy him catching her even more.

She laughed, loud enough that she knew he'd hear. Across the distance, she heard his challenging roar, and it made her grin like a loon.

But her joy took a hit of cold water to the face when she realized the other males in the area weren't heading toward her anymore. They were circling around in front of Nick, getting between her and her chosen mate.

Oh, that was not going to happen.

She took off through the thick forest. Even in human form, she wove easily through the trees and over the heavy undergrowth. This part of the central Appalachians was frequently used for the Runs because they weren't likely to be interrupted by human hunters or hikers. Her feet had a thick padding that made moving over the uneven ground as easy as if she were in tiger form, and kept her feet from getting too cold in the snow while she was moving.

But even at top shifter speed, she reached Nick only after he was completely surrounded by other males.

"Don't you dare," she roared, charging into the middle of the tension.

The males spun to face her, their scents carrying varying levels of confusion and aggression, lust, and anger.

"This is none of your concern, Tatiana," Fredrick, one of the males who'd run for her before, growled. "We're just getting rid of an unwanted intruder."

"He's here at my request."

That earned her a whole host of growls and shocked stares.

"What the hell are you talking about?" Fredrick continued speaking for the group.

"I want him here," she said, her voice low and deep. "He's allowed to run. You aren't allowed to stop him."

Nick kept silent, his attention on the males circling him, his body relaxed and at the ready. He was in human form—they all were at the moment—but some of the other males started to shift to their tiger forms even as Tiana moved to stand next to Nick.

"Get out of the way, Tatiana," Fredrick said. "You don't want him. He's crazy. Just like his father."

"Back off, Fredrick," she snapped. "I. Want. Him. Here."

"If he can fight us all off, he can stay." Fredrick kept his gaze on Nick. Nick stared back, still silent.

"No. Damn it, you're not allowed to fight. That's the fucking point of the Run."

"Get out of the way, Tatiana. We don't want you hurt."

More growls rose from the surrounding males, some tiger, and some human. Tiana felt a scream of rage and frustration rising in her throat.

Nick picked that moment to speak. "Stand to the side, Tiana," he murmured. "I've got this."

"There are thirty of them," she said over her shoulder. "No way am I letting you fight them all on your own."

"I can handle them."

The confidence in his voice sent another jolt of lust

through her, but she shook her head. "I know. But you don't have to handle them alone."

"I won't be."

She blinked and turned to look at him. Behind him, four males stepped from the trees, lining up at his back. She blinked, realizing two of the four looked a lot like Nick, though younger. His brothers. One of the four was Alexis' husband, Victor Romanov. She sniffed, taking in the scents of all four. The one she didn't immediately recognize had a familiar scent…Maxim Rudikov? He was a good friend of Mikhail, the youngest Chernikov, so it probably was him.

Nick glanced at her and winked before focusing on the others again.

She grinned.

"There's still a lot more of us," Fredrick said. He glanced at Victor and snarled. "He's even damaged."

Victor raised his brows, a slight smile hovering on his lips.

Nick said, "Outside of the fact that his wife would kill you if you managed to somehow hurt him, do you really think Alexis' mate is someone to take lightly?"

Victor's smile grew, and showed teeth.

Fredrick glared, but he took a step away from Victor, a telling gesture. "We can take you five," he snarled to hide his retreat.

"You're gonna have a harder time taking all eleven of us," said a new voice from the trees.

Tiana almost whooped as all six of her brothers entered the area to stand at her back. She couldn't seem to stop her grin.

Fredrick's brows snapped down in a scowl. Then he looked at Tiana. "What the hell is this?"

"Family. Making sure their sister gets her Run without anyone breaking the rules."

"Bitch," he snarled at her. "You're nothing but a frigid bitch."

"Then why the fuck have you been chasing me for three years, you asshole?"

He took in her body, naked so she could shift freely if she chose, and snorted. "You've got fantastic tits. The only reason any man would want you."

A series of growls rose behind her and next to her. Nick, fists clenched at his sides, took a step toward Fredrick. She put her hand out to stop him. "Don't. He's not worth it."

"Neither are you," Fredrick said, and spit in her direction.

She raised her brows in surprise. Then laughed. "You're never going to get a mate that way."

Fredrick's expression darkened and to her complete surprise, he lunged at her, so suddenly and with so much anger, she didn't have time to think.

She still watched it all in a weird kind of slow motion. Fredrick raising his hand to hit her, Nick stepping in and stopping the man's fist mid-swing, the roars and growls that rose to deafening levels. Instinct moved her even though her brain had stopped working. She stepped forward and punched Fredrick squarely in the center of his face, a roundhouse that broke his nose and dropped him to his knees.

In the silence that followed, Tiana blinked at what she'd just done. Fredrick covered his face with his free hand—Nick still had one of his arms wretched up over his head—and blood poured from between his fingers.

"Don't hit girls," Tiana said into the silence. "It's rude."

Someone behind Nick made a choking noise. Tiana glanced back to see Victor patting one of the Chernikov brothers on his back as he coughed into his hand.

When she looked back at Nick, he was grinning at her. Despite his unwavering hold on Fredrick's hand, his full attention was on her. She grinned back.

Then she faced the rest of the males. "Anyone else want to argue Nick's right to be here?"

A lot of feet shuffling and quiet chuffing answered her, but no one stepped forward to take up the fight.

Ethan put a hand on her shoulder and squeezed. "Run, little sister. We've got these guys."

She smiled back at him, then looked at Nick, her grin turning wicked. She turned on her heels and took off into the forest.

Nick was the only male to follow.

Thrill, adrenaline, lust, and love pushed her to lead Nick on a merry chase. She didn't make it easy, testing him, making him prove his worth, though she already knew he was worth the world to her. She'd never had a Run like this, never been able to experience the joy and excitement of having a male she *wanted* tracking her through the trees.

For a moment, she lost him. She pulled to a stop and circled, sniffing and sensing for him. A split second after she picked him up again, he pounced, catching her up from behind and making her squeal in delight.

He growled against her throat, then bit her shoulder, a light but firm nip that made her thighs clench.

"You came," she said, grinding back against him.

"I intend to, yes."

She laughed. "You're here."

"I couldn't stay away." He trailed his lips over her throat, up to the sensitive skin under her ear, then he scraped his teeth over her earlobe.

She shivered in his arms. "You brought backup."

"So did you."

"Think that makes us pretty smart."

He chuckled but didn't stop his exploration, moving to the other side of her neck. He cupped her breasts and squeezed until she was writhing against him. His erection was thick and hard against her ass.

"I've missed you," he said, his voice harsh.

"I've missed you, too. I'm not sure what I would have done if you'd decided to stay away."

He pinched her nipples hard enough to make her moan.

"Never staying away again, Tiana. You're stuck with me now."

"Oh. That's the sweetest thing you've ever said to me."

He turned her to face him and kissed her, hard and hot and with so much need, Tiana melted into him. *Mine mine mine mine mine.* The chant continued through her head as she ran her hands over his hard body, exploring all the delicious skin and muscle, laying claim to him as she hadn't dared to before. He was here, they were following the rules —finally—and she would be able to keep him now.

She ignored the fact that she still had to get pregnant. That seemed a minor concern compared to the larger obstacle of getting Nick to run. Now, together, they could do anything.

She dropped to her knees and took his cock into her mouth, hungry to taste him, delighting in the sounds he made as she slid over him, swallowing him. Her estrous drove her hard, making her frantic with desire, and with Nick she felt no need to hold back, no shyness, no hesitance. She savored and took and tasted and kissed to her heart's content. When he lifted her, first from her knees and then higher, she wrapped her legs around his waist and welcomed him, opened to him.

He slid into her easily, she was so wet with wanting, and filled her up so completely she thought her heart might burst. They came together fast, hard, pounding, a rhythm that answered the tension and uncertainty of the last week and a half, releasing the doubt. She screamed when her first orgasm took her, rejoicing in the sound of their lovemaking echoing in the trees. When he came, she tightened her legs around his hips and hugged him with her whole body, holding him as he pumped into her. Even as her body settled a little, her heart continued to pound with a combination of contentment and excitement unlike anything she'd known before.

"I love you," she said against his temple. "Thank you for facing the others, for being here."

He eased back to hold her gaze, his green eyes dark in

the moonlight. "You're worth fighting for, Tiana. I'll fight for you for the rest of my life if I have to."

"We'll fight together," she said, holding his face in her hands so he could see her intent.

"Together," he agreed and kissed her.

CHAPTER EIGHTEEN

Because there was snow on the ground, they made
their way to the cabin set aside for couples during the
Run. Tiana had barely noticed the cold for most of the night
—her estrous pumping her naturally warm temperature up
even higher—but she was happy to move inside, to the
comfort of a large, soft bed.

They spent the rest of the night talking, making love,
and talking more. An intimacy Tiana had never experienced
with any other tiger came easily with Nick. He told her
about his meeting with the werewolf Adam. She offered her
services to Adam's sister as a marketing consultant. Nick
asked her more about her work, and they talked more about
his. They told good stories from childhood and discussed
the hazards of having brothers.

As dawn approached, she finally found the courage to
admit her deepest fear to him—that she was damaged in

some way and that was why she hadn't been able to connect with anyone.

"There's nothing wrong with you," he insisted.

"I guess I was just waiting for you."

With the winter dawn still two hours away, the cabin's interior was lit only by a low burning fire, covering the single, open room in dark shadows. The shadows made his sharp features stand out more.

"I… I saw you six years ago," he said, slowly.

"What are you talking about?"

"Six years ago, I saw you at the elders' compound. Caught your scent."

She felt like she'd been slapped with a pillow—enough of a shock to make her blink, but she was too confused to actually feel anything else yet. "What? Why didn't you talk to me?"

"I knew I'd return to the Run for you, but no tigress ever wanted me. I didn't want to face that from you, so I left. But…you've been in my thoughts ever since."

"For six years?"

He shrugged.

She remembered his scent being vaguely familiar when she'd first caught it four months ago. Had she noticed his scent years earlier? Had her tiger picked him way back then? She felt her mouth drop open and closed it with a snap.

"What?" he asked, his fingers idly combing through her hair.

"I think I caught your scent back then. I really have been waiting for you all this time."

He frowned. "No. That's not possible. You never noticed me, and I got away from you as fast as I could."

"My tiger recognized you, even if I didn't. You've been the only one for me for years. No wonder no one else would do." She glared. "You ass. I thought I was broken."

"Hey, it's not my fault. Blame your tiger."

She growled. Then she let her shoulders relax. "I guess I can't be too mad. My tiger does have very good taste."

He snorted.

"I just wish we hadn't wasted so much time. We could have been together from my first Run."

"I didn't know that at the time. Experience had taught me otherwise."

"If you'd given me the chance, I would've convinced you."

"That's what I was always afraid of."

She frowned and touched the furrows that had formed between his brows. "I know you didn't want to come back to the fighting, but…is there something else?"

He let out a sigh. "The fights were an excuse, an easy excuse. But not the real reason I've never tried hard to get a mate."

She watched emotion flow over his face, things she couldn't decipher. She pulled in his scent but even that didn't give her a clear idea of what was wrong.

"I ran away from you six years ago because I knew from the first hint of your scent that I'd fall hard for you. I couldn't risk it."

"Why?"

He met her gaze. "Everyone has always said I'm just

like my father. And they're right," he said. "I am my father's son."

"No. You're not like that at all," she insisted. "How could you think that?"

"Beyond the fact that I see him in the mirror every time I look? Tiana, I know, deep down, I have more of him in me than I'd like."

She shook her head. "Nick… I don't know your father. I can't make a personal comparison. But…"

He stopped her with a gentle finger on her lips. "When I fought the werewolf alpha for you, when I thought you were in trouble, I finally understood my father, really understood what had happened to him. I don't even remember the end of that fight, not clearly. I went somewhere dark. If I lost you, I know I'd go there again."

She didn't want to make light of his fears, but she couldn't imagine Nick going on a killing spree and abandoning his children, even if he were grieving. "Two things. First, you're not going to lose me—not for a long time and not if I have any say in the matter."

He smiled a little. "You can't make any promises."

"I know life is precarious, but I won't be going anywhere willingly. You're stuck with me now."

"I'm not complaining."

She kissed him, then said, "Second, I'm going to demand you make a promise to me. When we have children, *if* something happens to me, your first concern needs to be our kids—they'll need their father. You understand that better than anyone. So you have to promise me that you'll be there for them, look after them, for me."

He swallowed visibly. "I'm not sure I can make that promise."

"Why?"

"I..." He blinked and frowned. Then he sat up and scowled at the dark bedroom walls.

She studied him by that low firelight, the flickering of orange and red dancing across his features. Part of her wanted to launch into more talk, to fix this problem so he stopped worrying. But as with returning to the Run, he had to make this promise to her of his own free will. She held her tongue, barely, and waited while he thought seriously about what she'd asked of him.

Finally, he looked back at her. "I'm worried I'll break this promise, Tiana. I don't want to. Losing our father the way we did was as bad as losing our mother. We were essentially orphaned. I never want to do that to my own children, which is why I never thought to have any. But with you, I want the family, the future, the hope. So...I will promise you that if anything happens to you, I will stand by our children first and foremost. I'll make sure they're looked after and have my support. I can't promise I won't want to lose myself in grief. But I'll...I'll try, for you."

She let out a breath and hugged him. This wound of his, his family history, would take time to heal. He wouldn't be convinced he wasn't his father overnight. He'd have to learn to trust himself as much as she trusted him. But they had time—she had time to work through his fears with him. And they would.

"Now," she said, leaning back and cupping his face in her hands. "I have to warn you."

"What is it?" He sat up a little and held her shoulders.

"I want five kids."

"Five?"

"At least." His eyes widened so much she grinned. "I want a huge family, Nick. Does that scare you?"

He met her gaze and shook his head. "The only thing that scares me now is losing you."

"You won't."

"What if, after years with me, you get tired of me and kick me to the curb?"

"Don't do anything to make me kick you to the curb," she said very seriously.

His expression relaxed and he smiled, a sexy little half-smile, as he pulled her close. "Five kids, huh?"

"At least. I'm used to a big family. I like a big family."

"I can get used to that. With you."

She kissed him and hugged him close. "I love you, Nick."

He eased back and stared at her a long moment. "I've been afraid to love for a long time. I'm still terrified I'll do something… But I love you, Tiana. I'm prepared to take the risk. For you. For a future with you."

He kissed her again and made love to her again, and Tiana's world fell into place.

The last day of their three days together, Nick woke to Tiana sitting up in bed next to him. He loved waking up next to her. He wanted to do this for the rest of his life.

He intended to do this for the rest of his life. Only one thing would delay that.

"I'm going to hate saying goodbye to you," he said. "Not sure I'll be able to wait until your next cycle to see you again. I will, but it's going to be tough."

She frowned a little. "This is my last Run, Nick. I thought I made that clear."

He sat up, a thread of panic tightening his muscles. "I don't understand. I thought… You said you loved me. You want five children."

"I do." She cupped his cheek. "But I'm not running anymore. Three years is enough."

"Tiana, until you're pregnant, you have to run or we can't be together."

She gave him a funny look, then a soft smile. "Take a deep breath, Nick."

He did, panic still firing adrenaline through his body. He focused on her delicious scent, the way their two flavors mixed together to form a perfect combination, then caught something…more. Something a little flowery, light, earthy. Impossible to describe. Even his tiger wasn't sure what the added scent was immediately.

He frowned at her, and her smile grew.

"Nick, you silly man, I'm pregnant."

His mouth actually dropped open. Surprise had him blinking at her for long moments before what she said sank in. "Pregnant? Already? But…that never happens."

"Told you we had good chemistry."

"It takes cycles, sometimes years, even with couples

who are in love. Mitch's friend Max chased his tigress for two years before they got pregnant. How…?"

"My body obviously knows what's best for her. I knew, the instant I caught your scent, you were the only man for me. My tiger has apparently known this for six years."

She scowled a little, and he grimaced. If he'd had any idea she'd scented him all those years ago… Well, he'd probably still have stayed away. He was thrilled Tiana was more stubborn and single minded than he was—something he hadn't actually thought possible—because otherwise, he wouldn't have this beautiful future sitting in bed with him.

"We've just proved we're perfect for each other," she continued. "In a way no one will ever be able to dispute."

His heart thumped hard as the implications sank in. He didn't have to keep running for her. He was going to be a father. Tiana was pregnant. With his child.

"Marry me," he said, taking her face in his hands. "Marry me. Tomorrow."

She laughed and kissed him. "I'll marry you. But not tomorrow. I want all my family there. And yours. And Jane and Charlie and… Well, I think everyone in Eirene will want to attend. I want the reception at your diner. We'd better wait till it warms up a little, though, because the party will spill out into the streets."

"I can't wait that long."

"Don't worry. I'll be there. You're my mate. Now and always. The wedding will just be the party to celebrate it."

"I love you, Tatiana Loban-Gupta. I'll do my best to be a good husband for you. And a good father for our children."

"I know you will be. I've always known." She laughed and kissed him, and he hugged her close, savoring her delicious, perfect taste.

"Told you we were made for each other," she murmured against his mouth before diving into another kiss.

Nick had never been so thrilled to be proven wrong in his life.

Thank you for reading Her Tiger To Take.

**If you've enjoyed this book, keep reading for an excerpt
from book 5 in the Tiger Shifters Series,
To Tempt A Tiger.**

TO TEMPT A TIGER

EXCEPT TIGER SHIFTERS 5

CHAPTER ONE

Rose Callaghan growled at the knock on her front door. Damn it, she didn't have time for visitors right now. If it was someone selling something or…well, pretty much anyone but a doctor, she was going to slam the door in their face.

She considered ignoring the knock. Her daughter was hurting and she didn't want to leave Zoe alone when she was in pain. But Rose also didn't want someone pounding on the door and disturbing them more.

Grumbling kid-safe curses on the way to the entry, she considered trying the doctor again. Or maybe the ER. None of it had helped in the past. No drugs could alleviate Zoe's bouts of extreme pain. No tests had uncovered a cause. No specialist had ever been able to help.

After almost a year and a half of this, she was considering some unorthodox options, things that would make her family balk, but she was desperate. Seeing her beloved daughter in pain was infinitely worse than any pain she might experience herself, and she'd do anything to fix things.

The doorbell rang and Rose hissed a not-kid-friendly curse. She trotted to the door and threw it open, prepared to take the hide off the person disturbing her. Until she saw the man on her front step. She froze, her mouth open, her brain momentarily too stunned to work.

Vladimir Dubrovsky. The love of her life. The man she'd planned to marry.

The man who had accused her of cheating on him and left her when he found out she was pregnant.

Rose blinked as the reality of Vlad being on her doorstep sank in. He looked the same: dark hair, dark eyes, sharp, sexy features, the perfect mouth, and a body designed to make a woman's mouth water.

"Hello, Rose," he said. "I realize this is a little…unexpected."

His voice was still that deep rich octave that had always made her shiver. She released a loud breath.

"Unexpected?" She wanted to laugh. She grabbed his arm and jerked him inside. "Thank God. Get in here."

His wide-eyed shock might have given her some satisfaction if she wasn't so worried.

"Your daughter is sick," she said, dragging him into her living room. "The doctors can't tell me what's wrong. What did you pass on to her? This isn't anything from my side—we've run tests and done the research. You need to tell me everything about your family medical history."

Vlad stood in her living room staring at her, his head angled down slightly, his brow furrowed. He looked at her like she was speaking a foreign language.

Her patience didn't stretch this far. "Damn it, Vlad, snap out of it. I need your help. What the hell is wrong with our daughter? She's hurting and I have to stop it. If you have any information that will help, you need to tell me. Now."

"This isn't the reception I was expecting."

"I don't have time for that right now. Can you help or not? If not, get out."

He shook his head, like a dog shaking off water, and straightened. "May I see her?"

She hesitated. This man had abandoned them. She hadn't seen or heard from him in more than four years. She wasn't sure she wanted him around her daughter—even if he was Zoe's father.

But if he could help with Zoe's pain…

"Do you know what's wrong with her?" she asked.

"I might. Is the pain cyclical? It comes and goes? Does she complain her muscles and bones feel like they're stretching and aching? Has she ever said her body feels like it's coming apart?"

"Yes! The doctors have tried a bunch of stuff and none of it works."

"None of it would. May I see her?" he asked again.

This time Rose didn't hesitate. "Come on." If he could take Zoe's pain away, she might just be able to forgive him for breaking her heart. Maybe. She'd certainly stop wishing the torments of Hell on him.

At the entrance to Zoe's bedroom, she spun to face him. The move brought them up close, and for an instant, her breath caught. He still smelled like the most delicious thing ever, spice and musk and male. She pushed the thought aside and pointed a finger at him.

"Don't scare her or hurt her. If you do anything that pisses me off, you're out of here. I'm too scared and worried about her to put up with nonsense. Also, no cursing." She turned and walked into her daughter's brightly decorated, white and yellow room.

"Zoe. I have someone here to see you."

"No doctors." Zoe's frown was set, stubbornness in every cute, chubby little line of her face. Then her body jerked and she moaned.

Rose forgot about Vlad as she hurried to her daughter. "Baby, I'm here. I'm here. It's going to be okay. I promise." She swallowed and brushed her daughter's sweat soaked hair from her little face.

"Mommy, it hurts."

"I know, baby. We'll fix it."

"Zoe." Vlad's tone was soothing and soft. "My name is Vlad. I'm not a doctor. But I might be able to help you. Can I sit next to you?"

She glanced up at Rose, pain pinching the skin around her beautiful dark eyes—eyes that had always reminded Rose of Vlad. Rose nodded her approval.

Zoe looked at him. "You got a funny name."

He smiled, then very gently sat next to her on the bed.

"When the pain comes, does it feel like your skin is stretching?"

She nodded.

"Do you…do you see any images in your mind when the pain hits? Does anything pop up in your imagination?"

"Tigers."

He straightened and sucked in a sharp breath.

"What?" Rose asked. "What is it? Why are tigers significant?"

He ignored her questions and focused on Zoe. "I'm going to talk you through breathing and things to think about that should help ease the pain. Okay?"

Rose glared. Positive thinking wasn't going to help her baby.

"I want you to take a long, slow breath," Vlad coached.

"Can't. Hurts."

"I know. But this will help. I promise. One long deep breath, and imagine the way your arms feel when you feel good."

Zoe nodded as she tried to take a deep, stuttering breath.

"That's it. Good girl. Now close your eyes and concentrate on how your whole body feels when you feel good. How your two legs feel. What the shoes on your feet feel like. What it feels like to wiggle your toes against the inside of your shoes. Got it?" He looked up at Rose. "What's her favorite toy or game? Something that involves physical sensation."

Rose snatched up Zoe's special blanket and handed it to him.

"I want you to imagine feeling your blanket against your fingers," he continued to Zoe. "Do you remember what if feels like? Concentrate on the soft material against your skin."

"She sucks on the corner," Rose put in.

Vlad nodded. "Remember what the corner feels like against your lips, on your tongue. How the blanket feels when it touches your cheek."

As he talked in slow, rhythmic, soothing tones, Zoe's breathing evened out and the tight lines around her eyes and mouth eased. Her little body relaxed and her shoulders slumped.

"Feeling better now?" Vlad asked.

She opened her eyes and smiled. "Better. I tired."

"You rest, baby," Rose said. Vlad stood and Rose tucked Zoe into her bed, making sure she had her favorite blanket in hand. "I'll be in the living room if you need me."

She nodded, then looked up at Vlad, her dark eyes narrowing toward sleep. "Thanks for taking the pain away."

"You're welcome."

Rose felt tears pricking her eyes and sniffled them back. She didn't like Zoe seeing her upset, not so soon after an episode. She motioned to Vlad, and they left Zoe to sleep.

In the living room, Rose stood for a long moment just staring at the pale carpet and breathing deeply. She felt so drained she wanted to sleep, too.

But first, she had some things to discuss with Vlad. "Sit." She motioned to the couch. "You want something to drink?"

"No."

"Why are you here?" She dropped into a chair opposite the couch.

Vlad sat, his brow creased. "I'm not sure how to start."

"Let me start then by saying thank you for helping Zoe. If you can tell me how to do that, I'd appreciate it. Then you can leave again."

Vlad scowled. "I can't leave you."

"You did before."

"That's not what I mean. It's… This is a complicated story."

She raised her brows, too tired to argue with him about the past.

"I was expecting a different reaction to my being here."

"What?"

He shrugged. "I thought you might slap me."

"Maybe if Zoe hadn't been in the middle of an episode I would have."

His mouth lifted in a little half smile, and Rose's heart thumped hard. Damn him, how did he do that to her with just a smile? She hated him. It didn't make sense that she could feel anything else for him, especially not this longing.

"I should start with an apology," he continued.

She snorted. "Little late for that now."

"It's offered anyway."

"Why?"

He paused before saying, "I have reason to believe I was mistaken when I left."

She gave him a deadpan stare that would have shriveled a weaker man. "Really? What led you to this epiphany?"

"Discovering I had a half sister I didn't know about. Seeing the state Zoe was just in confirmed my suspicions."

"How does you having a sister make you rethink your accusation that I cheated on you?"

"I was telling you the truth when I said we couldn't have kids. At least, the truth as I knew it. You and I should not have been able to conceive a child. Because of that, I was left with no alternative but to think you'd been with another man."

"We did have a child. I didn't cheat on you."

"I believe you now."

"Why now? Why didn't you believe me then? Why were you so convinced we wouldn't be able to have kids? You hadn't had a vasectomy and there was nothing wrong with me."

All those years ago, he'd been very clear about the fact that they wouldn't be able to have children naturally. He'd always seemed sad when he talked about not having kids, and she really wanted them. But, he'd told her, if she wanted them, she either needed to find someone else, or they'd have to consider alternatives like adoption. She'd been prepared to adopt. So long as she and Vlad were together, it hadn't matter how they built their family. At least not to her.

When she'd realized she was pregnant, she'd been thrilled, thinking whatever Vlad had been told about his ability to reproduce had been a mistake. She'd expected him to be as excited as she was, and she'd even deluded herself into thinking he'd propose then and there.

But he hadn't proposed.

He fisted his hands against his thighs. "You're not going to believe what I'm about to tell you. But for Zoe's sake, you need to know the truth. Then we need to go somewhere safe for a few weeks."

"Whoa, whoa, whoa. What are you talking about? Why would we need a 'safe' place?" She straightened in her seat, her exhaustion vanishing.

"I'm pretty sure my brothers have figured out…about Zoe."

"Vlad, you are as clear as mud right now. What the hell?"

"Okay. The truth." He leaned forward and met her gaze steadily. "I'm a tiger shapeshifter. Tigers and humans aren't supposed to be able to have children. That's why I thought you'd cheated on me. Then I learned about my sister. Her father is human, but her mother—my mother—was a tiger. Turns out, it is possible for me to have children with a human woman. And if my brothers learn Zoe is my child, they will try to kill her."

Look for To Tempt a Tiger (Tiger Shifters 5) out now!

AUTHOR'S NOTE

To the bit of literary license I took in this book. Those of you familiar with Colorado have no doubt realized there is no such place as Eirene on the road between Vail and Denver. There's no Eirene, Colorado period. I hope you'll forgive me for the invention. Typically, I like to stick to real locations and places that actually exist. But I wanted to do something very specific with Eirene, I wanted to build a certain kind of town, and I didn't want to take that kind of license with a real place and risk insulting someone's home. Thank you for understanding. We will be seeing Eirene again in the series, so I hope you enjoyed your visit there.

As a bit of trivia, I named the town Eirene after the Greek goddess of peace. I thought that was very fitting for a town of misfit toys looking for a place to belong.

ACKNOWLEDGMENTS

I got the opportunity to work with new editors on this book and I want to thank them very much for all their help in bringing this story to its full potential. My sincere thanks to Jena at Practical Proofing for her excellent insights. And a huge thanks to Becky and the crew at Hot Tree Editing for their sharp eyes and wonderfully supportive comments.

Additionally, I would like to thank my fellow writerly cohorts: Kemberlee Lugo, Stacey Agdern, Leanna Renee Hieber, Mala Bhattacharjee, Elizabeth K. Mahone, Lise Horton, Hope Tarr, Stacey Klemstein, and Linnea Sinclair. A huge thank you to you all, my dear friends.

Thank you to all the readers who keep returning to the Tiger Shifter world. I am, as always, truly grateful to you for your support.

Finally, I must thank my beloved family, who continue to put up with me when I'm in the midst of deadlines and mayhem. I couldn't continue without the love and support of my husband and two beautiful boys. I also have to thank my parents and sister—they know why.

Thanks!

BOOKS BY KAT SIMONS

TIGER SHIFTERS SERIES

1 - Once Upon a Tiger

2 - Along Came a Tiger

3 - Here There Be Tigers

4 - Her Tiger To Take

5 - To Tempt a Tiger

6 - Down Will Come Tiger

7 - To Catch a Tiger

8 - What a Tiger Wants

9 - Taming Her Tiger

Tiger Shifters Series Vol 1 (Books 1 - 3)

Tiger Shifters Series Vol 2 (Books 4 - 6)

ABOUT THE AUTHOR

Kat Simons earned her Ph.D in animal behavior, working with animals as diverse as dolphins and deer. She brought her experience and knowledge of biology to her paranormal romance fiction, where she delights in taking nature and turning it on its ear. After traveling the world, she now lives in New York City with her family. Kat is a stay-at-home mom and a full time writer.

For more on Kat and her future books:

Website: http://www.katsimons.com
Newsletter: http://eepurl.com/0xQQL